Three Winds Blowing

Three Winds Blowing

A NOVEL

RANDY WILLIS

TABLE OF CONTENTS

Prologue

October 1, 1852, could be called a glorious day in Evergreen, Louisiana. A little bit of crispness still hung in the air that hinted at the colder weather yet to come. Even at noon, there were only a few clouds to be seen, but enough to create a comfortable breeze, which carried the tantalizing aroma of Sunday's chicken and fresh ham for a supper on the grounds of the church near a huge brush arbor.

The rather gaunt, ninety-four-year-old preacher, Joseph Willis, made his way out of Bayou Rouge Baptist Church with the help of the menfolk in his family. It had been a morning racked with joyful emotion as Joseph had publicly blessed his grandson, Reverend Daniel Hubbard Willis Sr., to carry on his church-plantin' and gospel-sharin' call. Each step he took seemed lighter to him, now that he had passed off the torch of his ministry. He had no doubt that Daniel would become a mighty man of God. He had known that since not long after his birth in 1817, for Joseph had watched him carefully and listened to his words spoken to others. They were filled with kindness and a godly wisdom far beyond his youthful years. Joseph thought for a long time that he was a blessed man, and this morning served as confirmation in his heart.

With some careful planning and a few grunts, they were able to hoist Joseph into the hospital wagon that was headed back to Lemuel's home in Blanche, Louisiana, where Joseph now lived. But, Joseph had decided he wished to spend a few days at his ole home place in Babb's Bridge on Spring Creek, so the wagon rolled in that direction. Daniel now owned the home, and it would be an opportunity for Joseph to visit with his family and friends from days long since past. Little did he know that his great-grandson, Daniel Jr., would use the time to draw a wealth of information from him that would forever change his life and flood Joseph's mind with memories long since passed.

There were several family members present that morning, and Joseph felt an overflowing love for them all. Being the patriarch of the huge family had given him the opportunity to celebrate the birth of his nineteen children, the legacy of love passed to his grandchildren, and even his great-grandchildren. He had shared in the joys of new babies coming into the Willis family and seen many tears shed in the cemeteries where young and old had been laid to rest.

As all found their places in the various wagons and buggies, Lemuel took the reins. Daniel tucked the traveling quilt around Joseph's legs. Daniel's wife, Anna, had sewn the quilt using the leftover scraps of material from her children's clothes. Daniel and Joseph both remembered several of the prints and plaids. With each loving stitch, she thought of another Joseph from the Bible. His father had giving him a coat of many colors. Gently, Daniel wrapped Joseph in family memories.

"Father, can I ride with you and great-grandpa?" The voice of thirteen-year-old Daniel Hubbard Willis Jr., known as Dan, could be heard from a distance as he brought a cup of strong coffee with chicory to the wagon for Joseph. Young Dan had been scoutin' out his favorites—juicy peach cobbler and dewberry pie.

Daniel glanced at Joseph, who responded with a slight nod. The wagons, some pulled by horses and some by mule teams—even some by oxen—began their steady and plodding journey down the worn path toward Babb's Bridge. The two grassless wagon ruts showed years of ongoing use. Joseph was inwardly pleased with the wear on the road. He called those ruts *love tracks* because it meant there were many people coming and going from God's house.

Silence dominated during the first mile, and Daniel watched Joseph with an eagle eye. He had watched his grandfather change, and it was especially noticeable today. He had lost some weight, and his cheeks were slightly more sunken. His once smooth face now sagged with many wrinkles. The hair that had been so very dark now appeared totally grey. Even his once-strong hands had become gnarled with age. But, one thing had not changed, and that was Joseph's memory. With alert but dimmed eyes, he still watched everybody and could take any experience and turn it into a teachable moment. Finally, Daniel broke the silence: "Grandpa, are you comfortable?"

"Daniel, there's not a wagon known to man that's comfortable to me, but the joy of bein' with my family makes this ride easier today."

"Grandpa, are you too tired to talk? To tell one of my favorite stories?"

Joseph Willis's face produced a faint smile, and Daniel could read his eyes very well. It was story-tellin' time, and Daniel knew in his heart that these times were to end soon. After all, Grandpa was the oldest man he knew, so he was especially attentive to his beloved grandfather and teacher along life's rocky road. With an all-knowing little laugh, Joseph asked, "Now, Daniel, which story might that be? I've told you all of 'em by now."

"I want to hear about the sandbar fight again and how your friend Jim Bowie became famous. I want Dan to hear that story, too. Tell 'im how you were late 'cause of some green-broke molly mule. Someday, Dan wants to travel to east Texas, buy cattle, and be a cattleman. He already knows the Alamo story, but he hasn't heard *how* Jim Bowie came to be known by folks far and wide. He wants to write it all down in his diary."

Grandpa remained silent for a while as if trying to put all the pieces together in his mind. He took a deep breath and began looking intently at Dan.

"Dan, the wind of freedom first drove me from my home in North Carolina to the banks of the Mississippi, but it was a mighty, rushing wind that compelled me to swim the turbulent waters of the Mississippi

River, in 1798, on my mule into the Louisiana Territory, while the dreaded Code Noir forbade me from doing so. The Territory was a land rooted in tradition and chivalry.

"It was a land that had lost its innocence. Here, I soon discovered a third wind blowing: the wind of war fueled by human bondage.

"Dan, it's an evil wind caused by this slavery issue—and I fear you and our family will be left to deal with the destruction to our property and our way of life it will most surely bring. I saw this wind blow in 1775 and its ruination when I fought with the Swamp Fox Francis Marion in 1780 in the Pee Dee River swamps of South Carolina. The cost of freedom was high then, but well worth it. Mark my words, if war comes to Louisiana, the cost will be much higher than the politicians tell ya."

Lemuel stopped the wagon to hear too. Joseph paused and studied their faces carefully. "We have all embraced the first two—*the winds of freedom and the spiritual wind*. But, my question to all three of you is this: how will you deal with the third wind, the *wind of war*?" Again, there was more silence as he stared at them. He had a way of looking past the eyes, right into the soul. "How you answer that question will determine how you deal with the war that I fear we are gonna have soon."

Silence covered the wagon like a thick blanket.

"Now, what was the question? Oh, let me tell ya the story of my friend, Jim. Here's what I remember."

Narrative

1

September 19, 1827

VIDALIA, LOUISIANA

For six long days I had ridden my old mule, Josh, from Bayou Chicot to Vidalia, Louisiana. We were to cross the Mississippi River there on a barge and then head on to Bethel Baptist Church in Woodville, Mississippi. I was really lookin' forward to seeing my old friends at the church and meetin' new ones. We arrived Wednesday mornin' and went directly down to the river's edge to catch a barge. When I got there, the dock was empty. There was one plump old man sittin' on a crate with a fishin' pole, surrounded by some hungry, brown pelicans.

"Where's all the barges?" I asked. "I need to cross to Natchez today, 'cause I have a church meetin' a little later this week."

The barge tender laid down his pole, got up slowly, and walked in my direction. He was a rough one and spoke with gruffness in his voice. "Well, you can wait 'til they come back tonight and leave in the mornin', or . . . you can swim it, mister. Ain't no barges to be had *today*. Nope, no barges! Some crazy men from Alexandria took all the barges this mornin'. Yup, they's *crossin' the river*."

"I know, you already told me that they went across to the other side."

I could tell he was irritated, 'cause his face got real red. "No, they's gonna fight it out. Ya know, a duel, an affair of honor."

5

I told 'im, "Oh, I heard some talk about a possible fight a couple weeks ago. Didn't know it would come to this."

"Yup, some men stayin' at the Alexander House named Wells, Cuny, Bowie, and McWhorter, or somethin' like 'at. They's headed for the sandbar in the oxbow of the river, just north of Natchez on the other side, to fight it out with a guy named Maddox. Yup, they're crossin' the river today."

There was only one name that I recognized. My heart began to pound. "Bowie . . . Jim Bowie?"

"Yup, you know 'em?"

Sweat broke out on my forehead, and I had a real sick feelin'. "I've got to get there *this* mornin'."

"Well, you ain't gonna git there, 'less you plan on swimmin' it on that old mule of yours, and that's just plain impossible." He pointed to the mighty, rollin' river. "I hear'd it's only been done once, and that was by some crazy young preacher, but that was before my time here at the dock."

I couldn't believe that anyone was still talkin' about that swim I took with my old mule, Josh. Lookin' up with a grin, I told 'im, "I was crazy then, and I'm just crazy enough to do it again." He looked at me as if he'd just heard a dog talk. I stopped and sized up Josh. Reality struck me hard when I saw 'im. Josh had done me well, but he really was too old now, and I knew he couldn't swim it again. Wasn't sure I could, either.

Collectin' my thoughts wasn't easy. I just knew I had to get there. "Where can I buy a mule colt? A molly will work, too. Quickly, tell me! Please."

"Go down that street a stretch, and you'll find a horse trader. You can git a good mule there, but be careful. If you got *any* horse sense, use it well. Ya know what I mean?"

"Sure do," I muttered as I walked away, "all too well . . . some of 'em are like some preachers I hear tell of."

I found the place without any trouble and went up to the trader.

"Mornin'. Do you have any mules for sale? I gotta get 'cross that river today!" He looked at me with curiosity and seemed to study me as he walked to the stall. After fumblin' with the gate, he led out the only mule in the stable.

"This here's a good molly mule. She's a good'un', and she'll give ya some good years. She's as fit as a fiddle."

Reluctantly, I continued to explain my travels and preachin' and how I needed a broke mule, not just a green-broke mule, 'cause I had no time for trainin'. I never had used my bein' a preacher to get someone's favor, although others did, but this time I just had to, for it was a matter of my friend's life. I'd have to ask God for forgiveness later. He just kinda smiled, nodded his head the whole time I was talkin', and finally said, "Yup, here's the one for you. I will sell her to you for a good price, 'cause of you bein' a preach'r man."

His smile brought me little comfort. He acted as though he had not heard a single word I'd said. I took the mule from 'im and snubbed her to a nearby tree. After prying her jaws apart and lookin' at the lines on her teeth, I figured her to be 'bout three years old. I walked 'round and touched her and even tried to spook her. She didn't respond except to look at me with her big, brown eyes as if to say, "What's your problem?" When I climbed on her back, she did not flinch—*too much.*

He tried to sell her for the price of a broke mule that had just won a horse race, but I made a deal with 'im and paid a reasonable price, for a green-broke mule, that is. It didn't take me long to settle on a name. She kinda looked like a *Sally*. She looked older than her years 'cause of her flea-bitten, gray-hair coat, so I named her Ole Sally. I asked 'im to keep Josh there 'til I got back the next week. I told 'im, "I'll pay ya, and he don't eat much."

The trader looked at Josh and grinned. "He's too old to even be a good steal." Josh backed his ears and brayed as if he had understood. We both chuckled.

My trip back to the waterfront was easy. The river between Vidalia and Natchez was narrower, but it was still a far piece to swim. Ole Sally was cooperative as we eyed the water near the barge dock. I took a deep seat, a faraway look, and kept my mind on that opposite shore. I remembered Rachel once tellin' me, "Joseph, no river is too wide if you want what's on the other side." I wanted my friend to live, but obviously Rachel had not seen the Mississippi. But, my friend's life was enough reason to try and swim the river 'gain.

After securing everythin' tightly on Sally's saddle and cinchin' her saddle up real tight, we waded into the warm, muddy water. At first it was sandy, but then we could feel the mud and plants almost as thick as a swamp. We walked until Ole Sally could no longer touch the bottom. Bein' free of that thick, weighty mud was a welcomed relief. She swam for a short distance, and then the current began to take over.

We had not gone far when Ole Sally's eyes widened, and she began to lunge frantically in the river. I tried my best to calm her down and couldn't see anything to bring her that much fear. My eyes skimmed the top of the water, and not far from us was a pair of water moccasins. I did not know *their* destination, but I knew that two of 'em meant extreme trouble for us, 'cause I could not keep my eyes on both of 'em as they circled while Ole Sally almost drowned us both.

Ole Sally was desperately fightin' to escape, and we started bobbin' and goin' under. She pulled me with her. I had to struggle to keep her movin' away from those snakes. As she came up, she snorted and made some horrible noise. I prayed. "Please, Lord, save us. Help us not to drown."

Under we went, into the murky water again. This time, I somehow got tangled in my rope when the piggin' string broke . . . the one that tied it to my saddle horn. I had to cut myself free with a little gift that Jim had given me months before. The swift current seemed to push at us from all directions. I could see the surface but could not seem to break to the top. Suddenly, I remembered why I was doin' this and found what little strength was left in me.

8

The fresh air in my lungs smelled mighty good. Not far away, Ole Sally came up, too. Her wide eyes said it all. I grabbed her tail and held tightly as she treaded water and moved forward. I think fear drove her to keep goin'. Thankfully, the moccasins were nowhere in sight. We both relaxed a lil' and kept movin' southward with the strong current. The only problem was that we needed to be goin' east, to the other side. It was almost by instinct that Ole Sally kept us goin' toward the far banks of the river. Eventually we came to the shallows on the other side and walked out—both of us exhausted.

There were quite a few onlookers as we came ashore. A weather-aged man rowed up in his li'l fishin' boat. "Hey, glad to see you made it. I thought you and that mule were goners. Sure looked like you both were gonna drown."

Bent over with my hands on my knees, all I could do was glance up at 'im and shake my head. "Not hardly—at least not today!"

✦ ✦ ✦

A puzzled thirteen-year-old face looked at Joseph intently. "But, Great-Grandpa, I don't understand why you would risk your life for someone who was gonna kill someone else?"

"Dan, ya gotta dance with the one who brung ya." Dan looked confused, and Joseph snickered and continued to explain. "I was loyal to my friend, Jim, and I wanted to stop this duel from happenin'. I believed that if I could get to 'im, I might be able to save his life, maybe others, too. Dan, if you want to have a friend, you got to be a friend. Oh, where was I? Let me tell you what happened next. . . . "

✦ ✦ ✦

By that time, it was mid-mornin'. I had to find the sandbar. The river's current had brought us further south than I had eyed earlier, so we needed to head back north to Natchez. It did not take us long to find a worn trail to the road, where I inquired about the remainin' distance. "You got to go a mile or so due north."

I no longer felt confident we'd make it by noon. Maybe I should have just gone up the river's edge, but it was not an easy journey with the rocks and trees. Ole Sally was able to keep a pretty good pace throughout the mornin', even though I knew she was worn out. So was I.

The September sun dried us quickly, and the thick, woodsy foliage kept us from bakin'. We passed many slaves on the road. Some were chained at the ankles, some at the neck, and some had wrist chains. There were several bare-backed men with hideous scars from the whip. There was a mixture of old scars and fresh, new ones. I could not help but wonder what they had done to receive the wrath of their masters.

As I passed 'em, I remembered my own days as a slave, but it was *nothin'* like this. My heart ached for 'em, and I quietly prayed for each man's well-bein'. Strangely, I only saw one woman on the road that day, and she was tied to the back of a carriage and bein' forced to run behind it—or be dragged. I especially prayed for her as I remembered my mother who had been a Cherokee slave.

My heart felt heavy when we finally reached Natchez. The town was crazy with talk about the fight. It was after 1:00, and I had missed it. No one was able to tell me any details, but I had that sick feelin' 'gain. We made our way through the town and headed toward the banks of the river. Three young men came runnin' toward me.

"Do you have news of the duel? Can you tell me if I'm on the right road?"

"Mister, the fight's over . . . two dead, and four bloodied terribly!"

My heart stopped. "Boys, do you know who died? Who was killed?" I climbed off Ole Sally and led her to the top of a grassy knoll. From there I could see the deserted sandbar and some barges halfway back 'cross the river. I got the impression from hearin' those young'uns talk that they had been hidin' in the woods and seen the whole thing happen.

I ask 'em, "What happened? Was Jim Bowie there?" They all seemed to talk at once. After listenin' carefully, I put some of the pieces together. There were two dead men, and one was Wright. I remember now that Jim had talked about 'im in very unchristian terms just a couple weeks before. A while back, Jim had asked Wright's bank for a loan, and they had denied 'im. Was it possible that Jim had killed Wright?

I sat on the grass and put my head down. Oh, how I had tried to stop that fight from happenin'! The boys continued talkin' amongst themselves about how the first two men had fired at each other and missed. They reloaded, shot again, and missed. They were ready to call it quits and even shook hands, but a man from one side came out and started yellin' at the other, sayin' somethin' like, "We're goin' to end our differences today."

Their story got a little cloudy in the tellin' about all the shootin' and stabbin', but the jist of what they'd seen was that the two secondaries had shot at each other and missed, and one hit Jim instead. He fell, they shot at each other 'gain, and one was shot in the chest and killed.

One boy said, "You should have seen this Bowie guy. He pulled out this big ole' knife! Didn't even have a gun. Came to a duel with no gun. He was fightin' mad and raised up to strike like a mean ole' rattlesnake. Even though he had a bullet in 'im, he went after the guy that shot and killed the other man. They were fightin' by hand, and he hit Bowie in the head with his gun so hard that the gun broke into pieces. Bowie used his knife on 'im."

It's a wonder that Jim was alive when they put 'im on the barge. He was shot to pieces and stabbed at least six or seven times. I had told Jim weeks before that if this happened it would not end well.

Dan patted Joseph's shoulder gently. "But, Great-Grandpa, how'd you know there might be a fight?

Joseph sat for a few moments, gazing at a flock of migrating Sandhill

Cranes. In his own mind, he had relived this encounter as if it were yesterday.

"Son, I was at Ezra Bennett's store a few weeks before—you know, the one at Eldred's Bend on Bayou Boeuf. I remember every single detail from that day. How could I ever forget?"

2

September 6, 1827

The sweat seemed to pour off my head, and even my hat could not sop it up fast enough. It was a hot, humid day like most every other day that summer. Certainly was glad to see Bennett's store just up ahead. I could sure use some water for me and my mule, Josh, along with a new bridle he would need for our trip over to Mississippi.

We were headed to Bethel Baptist Church for a revival meetin'. It was the first time I had been back since I was ordained, and I was really lookin' forward to preachin' there. It held a special place in my heart, being the first church I ever helped organize. I did not have long to think back on my early days as we broke through the clearin'.

The little store was right up ahead. Mind you, it was not a big store like you'd find in Alexandria, but I never cared for those big stores in Alex. My dear wife Hannah would always buy things we didn't need there. I was always amazed at how much he had in that little place, though. Some of the plantation owners and their families got their mail there.

I could always count on Bennett to fill my ears with the latest news 'round the area. A one-horse buggy was hitched to the rail outside. Openin' the door, I was hit with a musty coolness, for the building sat under some shade trees, but there was also the mixed aroma of cookin' herbs, leather, fresh bread, and maybe even a little sweet perfume. Bennett was helping a couple when I walked in.

"I'm helpin' Bowie here now, but I'll be with you in just a moment."

The customer with dirty-blond hair wiped his hand on his buckskins as he turned to look at me. His face lit up as he gave me a hearty handshake.

"Pastor Willis, what 'n the world ya doin' here? Oh, I want you to meet my fiancée, Cecelia Wells." He grabbed her by the hand and almost took her off balance as he dragged her 'cross the floor. "He's the one I was tellin' ya all about. He's the Baptist preacher man who gets churches started." Lookin' again at me with his big, grey eyes, he said, "We're gettin' married but haven't set a date yet. We'll let you know when it's gonna be. I would love to have you there and would be honored if you'd get us hitched."

"Slow down, Jim." I was in a full laugh by now. "I've not even had the honor of sayin' 'hello' to your bride-to-be." I removed my sweaty hat and turned to this unusually attractive young woman. I bowed and said, "Nice to meet you, Miss Wells. Sure hope you like huntin' and fishin', 'cause that's 'bout all he knows. Better yet, I hope you know how to cook all his catches." I could just tell they were a happy couple but couldn't resist givin' Jim a little jab. "Well, Jim, even an ole blind hog finds an acorn every now and then. Looks to me like you're marryin' up."

Everyone laughed, including Mr. Bennett.

"I think I can hold my own in that department," Miss Wells responded. She touched her ringlets to make sure none had moved too far from her tidy little bow. She held her ribboned bonnet by her side. Her stylish bonnet even matched the blue in her dress and eyes.

I think she picked up on our mood. She could tell that we had some catchin' up to do, and she began lookin' around at all of the merchandise while Jim and I stepped outside.

"Pastor Joseph, how are you? It's good to see ya again."

"So, you're finally getting married and settlin' down. It is about time, Jim."

"Wait, Pastor Joseph, I didn't say anything 'bout settlin' down. You know me, I'm always lookin' for a new adventure. Thinkin' Tejas might be my next one."

"Tell me what's happenin' 'round here. I have heard little pieces of gossip, but I know and trust your words."

"A scoundrel—a so-called doctor named Thomas Maddox—and his patrons have been sayin' a lot of disrespectful remarks about our womenfolk, and there's been some shootin's and stabbin's along the way, too. Some of it is political, but there sure is lots of tension. A friend of mine, Samuel Wells, is not going to put up with much more from those scoundrels. Their feud is gettin' ugly. The two of 'em will have to fight it out for this to end, and that'll be a *real* barn-burner, too!"

"Are you talkin' about an *affair of honor*? I don't think you should get involved in this."

Jim lifted his shirt to show a rather long scar on his ribs. "Too late, Pastor. You know Wright wouldn't give me a loan I needed, and he already wounded me once with his pistol. I want some satisfaction. The feud is heatin' up. I can't stop it. Anyway, ya know I don't have to carry a gun 'cause I just don't trust 'em. I only got this 'toad-stabbin' knife that I carry. Only important men with titles in front of their names, whether real or made-up, can fight it out like that. I'm just a guy who likes adventure." He ran his hand up and down the sheath in his belt as he spoke.

That look told me a whole lot more about his ability to protect himself than he let on. That is one thing I could say for Jim Bowie; he was hardheaded for sure, but he never talked about himself. That's what made me first like 'im.

"But you know what the Bible says about fightin' like that. Not only is it 'gainst man's law, but it's 'gainst God's law, too. I got a bad feelin' that nothin' good will come out of this."

"Pastor, just as your heart tells you I should not get involved in this, my gut tells me I *must*!"

The silence caused discomfort for both of us. Jim changed the subject and walked inside to collect his supplies and lady.

With Cecelia on his one arm and a parcel in the other, they walked to the buggy. "It was good seein' you again." He paused and looked at me. "I'll be careful. Ya won't read my name in any newspaper. Don't ya worry 'bout me." Cecelia was seated, and he climbed aboard. "I'm serious about the weddin', Pastor. I will be in touch with ya."

"That would be most enjoyable, my friend. And, Jim, I'm serious about this fightin', too. I don't see how it could possibly bring ya any honor. Think about it." I could not help but see the questions and concern written on Miss Wells's face. "There is also someone else to think about now, too." I nodded toward his fiancée.

3

Same Day

Just as they were ready to leave, a young man rode up on his lathered horse. He greeted us and seemed friendly enough, in an arrogant sort of way. He was talkin' even before he climbed out of his saddle. "Howdy, I'm Edwin Epps. You folks from 'round here?"

Jim climbed back down out of the buggy and did the introductions. "I'm Jim Bowie, and this here is my fiancée, Cecelia Wells. That guy over there is Preacher Joseph Willis. Nice to meet ya."

Young Dan interrupted, "Great-Grandpa, you mean Edwin Epps, your friend Solomon Northup's master? That Mr. Epps? I do want to hear more about 'im. Heard about what Mr. Epps did to his slave, Patsey. Is it really true that he made Solomon whip her after he was too tired to go on?"

"Yes, I'm 'fraid so, Dan. Keep in mind that when I met 'im at the store, he was only 'bout nineteen, and I figured even then that he had a lot of growin' up to do."

Anyway, Epps bowed to Miss Wells and shook our hands. He studied Jim's face for a few seconds and asked, "Are you the Bowie friend of Jean Lafitte? You the one that sold slaves down in N'Orleans with 'im? Someday I'm gonna have me a big cotton plantation, so I'll be findin' ya so as you can get me some niggers to work on my land. You live around here?"

I could tell Jim was uncomfortable, just by the way he looked at the ground and eyed 'im. Jim answered vaguely, "I travel a lot, but I don't live too far from here."

Epps looked directly at me and said, "Preacher, I heard of you, too! You're the one who gets churches started. You're friends with many of the plantation owners—*and their slaves*. Right?"

I nodded and wondered where he was goin' with this conversation. It did not take 'im long to explain.

"Yup, I'm gonna have me some slaves that dance to the whip and never give me problems. They won't be like those ignorant darkies down in the André and Meuillion Plantations. You hear'd what they did to 'em slaves, right?"

Jim and I stood there, tryin' not to flinch with his sordid details, and Miss Wells was now lookin' off in the distance. But Epps, he kept right on talkin'.

"Back in 1811, there was a bunch of 'em niggers, over 200 or so, who thought they could have a revolt and be free. What foolishness! They marched toward N'Orleans and were caught and rightly punished for bein' stupid. About forty-five were killed in the fightin', but I really like what they did to the ones they caught alive. They cut off their heads and put 'em on spikes, and stood 'em up along the Mississippi River levee for many miles. Served as a reminder for those other uppity niggers to mind their manners and obey their masters. Ain't heard of no more trouble since then." Epps scratched his head, "Oh, yeah, their leader . . . what was his name? Deslondes, or somethin' like that. Got his hands chopped off, and then they shot him in both legs and roasted him like a pig in some straw. What a great way for a nigger agitator to end his life! Don't y'all agree?"

I found it very difficult to speak to this young man after hearin' his hateful words, but I did manage to say this: "Mr. Epps, I'm not sure if you are serious about all this or not, but I can tell you in the eyes of the

Lord, you would never have such a right. To do so would be murder."

"Oh, yes I would, Preacher, 'cause they ain't got no souls, anyway. Surely, you know that!" His face was bright red with anger and hatred. "If you live 'round here, too, you have to know Peter Tanner, your fellow Baptist. He's a brother-in-law of William Prince Ford, a big plantation owner. I heard Tanner tell some plantation owners that the niggers had no souls."

I stood there shakin' my head and said, "Doesn't matter what Tanner says. That's not true."

Epps stopped for a moment, looked me square in the eyes, and said with a smirk, "Oh, that's right, Preacher, I forgot. You're mix't with Indian. You were once a slave, weren't ya? Well, least ya got *half* a soul."

I could feel my blood heatin' up, not 'cause of his words about me but because of his ignorance and disrespect to the Lord. I told 'im, "The Bible says, 'Let every man be a liar and God be the truth,'" and Mr. Epps, *this is wrong.*"

"You callin' me a liar, Preacher?" I watched 'im ball up his fists. "Oh, if you wasn't a preacher, I'd. . . . "

Jim, whose arms had been folded on his chest, let 'em drop to his sides. His hand was but maybe an inch away from his sheathed knife. "Well, Epps, I ain't no preacher, and I can tell you that I feel the same way as my friend."

Epps looked at that nine-inch knife in Jim's belt and thought 'bout Jim's growin' reputation. He seemed to lose some of that arrogance as he backed down. "Well, I ain't lookin' for no fight *today*."

We both waited to see who would speak the next words. I guess Epps knew he could not continue spittin' his venom and get the response he'd hoped for.

He tipped his hat toward Jim's fiancée. "It was a pleasure to meet you, Miss Wells. And good day to y'all." Epps went into Bennett's store and quickly returned. We were still silent as he mounted and left.

No one knew what to say. His words had the stench of vomit. I feared he might just grow up to be a real scary man on a mission. He was capable of heartless cruelty, even as a young man.

We said our goodbyes again and left. I turned one more time to Jim and shouted, "Do the right thing, Jim. Think 'bout it!"

Jim and Cecelia waved in my direction as their buggy disappeared around the bend.

I went back into the store and purchased a new bridle for Josh. It fit 'im well, and I wanted 'im to get used to it before our trip to Bethel Baptist.

So, that's the story of Jim Bowie's Sandbar fight, my boys.

The ride was silent for a while as they let the story sink in. Joseph finally coughed, cleared his throat, and spoke. "What do you think, boys?"

The old wagon rumbled along down the dusty road. Everyone seemed lost in thought as Joseph slipped gently into a quiet repose.

4

October 1, 1852

ON BAYOU BOEUF

SOUTHEAST OF CHENEYVILLE, LOUISIANA

Joseph had napped soundly for several miles and seemed to be stirring some under the elder Daniel's watchful eyes. "Grandpa, you doin' well?"

Lemuel stopped the wagon, and both Daniel and his son Dan helped Joseph to sit up. Lemuel had arranged for the hospital wagon and felt this would provide more comfort for his father. There was a raised pallet nailed to the floor of the wagon so it wouldn't move about. It had raised edges to keep him in place, almost like a cradle. The linseed-oiled cloth covering could be pulled over the frame to protect them all from any inclement weather.

Joseph took in all of the scenery. His face showed great peace as the broad-winged hawks flew overhead and blue jays screamed warnings of intruders to one another. Neither of the Daniels wanted to interrupt his reflection. After a few moments, Joseph looked around, carefully inspecting their location. He had traveled that road for decades. Not much had changed except the number of people traveling on it.

He spoke to Daniel with tender authority. "Up about half a mile is a perfect place to stay the night on Bayou Boeuf."

The elder Daniel was not going to rush his grandfather on this trip. He did not care if the three-day trip back turned into a week; he just wanted Joseph to be comfortable. The other family wagons had moved past for the sake of the teething babies and nursing mothers, and that just left the four of them to make their way at their own pace.

Within a short distance, Lemuel could see the exact place his father had described. The partially cleared area appeared to have had some overnight use in the recent past. There were big stones already set in a circle for their evening campfire. Some previously cut cedar stumps were set back a ways from the fire.

That night, they ate some fried chicken and biscuits with mayhaw jelly, along with some huckleberry pie that Lemuel's wife, Emeline, had slipped into the basket. Their conversation was rich with family chatter, and Joseph answered questions from the men. Young Dan sat and listened with great interest.

It was past sunset when there was a lull in the conversation, and Dan asked his great-grandfather, "Great-Grandpa, ya ever been scared?"

Everyone stopped and looked at Joseph, who was still eating his favorite pie, dewberry. "Son, that's a mighty interestin' question. What made ya ask that 'un?"

"Great-Grandpa, ya swam the Mississippi on a mule and fought with the Swamp Fox. Didn't ya ever feel afraid?" Dan had a curious look on his young face.

"There are lot of times I've been afraid, including those two, but I always knew the good Lord was with me." Joseph sensed that Dan was a little uncomfortable, so he decided to lighten the conversation. He thought for a few moments and spoke. "Son, did your father ever tell ya 'bout the time he was afraid when he got chased by a screamin' woman?"

Young Dan's mood changed quickly. He looked at Joseph and then at Daniel. "Father, did that really happen? Is Great-Grandpa pullin' my leg?"

Daniel's face got red, and he put his head down. Lemuel gave a hearty laugh.

Joseph's head turned slightly toward Daniel, even though he was still looking into the fire. "I thought by now you'd have already told 'im 'bout that screamin' woman you heard in the woods."

Joseph had obviously caught Daniel off guard. "Um, no sir, I hadn't told 'im that story, and didn't see any need for 'im to hear it from me. Ya know, Grandpa, you really don't have to share it. I'm sure there are plenty of others he'd like better. . . . "

Dan interrupted his father's protest. "Great-Grandfather, please tell me the story." Dan grinned. "It must be a good 'un if my father don't want me to hear it. Right?"

5

March 15, 1830

COCODRIE LAKE NEAR BAYOU CHICOT, LOUISIANA

Dan, years ago, your father and your grandfather Agerton had come for a visit, and we decided to take a fishin' trip. Your father was about your age, and we were campin' on the south side of Cocodrie Lake. Anyway, he slipped away and disappeared from the campfire one night and was gone for quite a spell. We were gettin' worried 'bout 'im, 'cause he didn't have a good sense of direction and, you know, his eyesight has never been that good. There was a big moon that night, but it was dippin' in and out behind the clouds."

"Was he *really* lost in the woods?" Dan asked as he stirred the fire with a green stick.

"Well, let's just say we couldn't find 'im. He didn't respond to our call, and he'd gone farther than he should have."

Young Dan had stirred up the embers enough to get a good look at both of their faces. Joseph seemed to enjoy every minute of this story, the elder Daniel not so much.

"My mind started playin' all kinds of tricks on me, and I knew there were some mean, large critters out there just waitin' for a tasty meal like Daniel. Also knew they might just come after our horses, too."

The elder Daniel interrupted his grandfather. "Are you sure you don't have another story you'd like to tell instead?"

Joseph shook his head firmly, "No, I kinda like this one." He turned back to young Dan. "Well, the time passed, and Daniel still didn't return. We were beginnin' to worry when all of a sudden, there was a screamin'—

24

the sound of which we'd never heard before. It sounded like a woman screamin' that was bein' hurt . . . and then another hollerin' commenced. We recognized the second sound as your father. He was yellin' at the top of his lungs and thrashin' through the blackjack and post oak. There was silence again, and then this blood-curdlin' scream filled the woods.

"Daniel musta caught sight of the campfire, and he ran as fast as he could to the clearnin'. Totally out of breath and half-silly with fear, he told us, 'There's some insane woman out in the woods! She's chasing me. Don't let her get me! Please save me! Get the gun and shoot her, 'cause she is really crazy! She's gonna hurt us all!'"

Joseph stopped for a moment and winked at Dan, then turned to speak to the elder Daniel. "Do you want to tell 'im who the screamin' woman was, or do you want me to?"

"Grandfather." Daniel hung his head. "You're havin' way too much fun with this to stop now. You go ahead and finish the story." While appearin' a little embarrassed, he still could not resist the opportunity to hear Joseph spin his yarn.

"We grabbed our weapons as we prepared to catch her. Her chillin' scream cut the silence again and made everyone uneasy, especially the horses. Your father was hidin' under the wagon by this time and could not be coaxed from his safe place."

The young Dan stopped his great-grandfather and asked, "Why didn't she just come out of the woods? Why, was she insane? What made her scream so bad?"

"Those are right good questions, Dan. You see, the 'screamin' woman' that chased your father in the woods was not a woman at all. It was a hungry panther who could smell a meal on four legs. She wasn't after your father. She wanted the horses. We could hear her claws hit the bark of a pine tree. She must have been climbin' high to watch and wait for a chance at our horses. She was a big one and probably had hungry kittens not far off."

Dan asked with all sincerity, "Were ya really gonna shoot and kill her?"

"Only if she had come too close to our family or the horses. She was hungry, and her instincts were strong, but her need for survival was greater. She did what came natural to her."

Everyone sat quietly, just staring into the fire. Young Dan seemed uncomfortable as he looked up into the nearby pine trees.

"So, we teased your father for quite some time, didn't we, Lemuel?" Joseph chuckled. "Over the years, I must 'ave thought of that night more 'an a dozen times." Joseph shifted his focus to the elder Daniel and asked, "did ya learn any lessons from that frightful night?" Joseph's curiosity urged him on. "Tell us."

Daniel laughed and rolled his eyes. "Grandfather, your story-tellin' is mighty excitin'."

Young Dan was on the edge of his stump, hugging his knees.

Daniel looked at his son and said, "Son, here's what I gained from my 'night of terror' in the woods. Me and the horses came close to bein' supper for a panther 'cause I wandered off from the safety of the group. When we stray away too far from our family, there's no tellin' what might happen. It's the same when we stray too far from the Lord. We aren't well-protected when we go our own way." Daniel stopped, and a great big grin seemed to cover his whole face. "And, as for that panther, it really did sound like a crazy woman screamin'. T'was the most chillin', scary sound I ever heard in my life."

Joseph couldn't stifle his amusement and again broke into a big laugh. They all laughed that night around the campfire, until they heard the scream of a panther in the distance. They looked at each other and one by one said, "Goodnight!" Except young Dan, who added, "I hope so."

Oh, how Joseph loved his Louisiana—the piney woods, the sights and sounds . . . lovely Louisiana. Paradise for a young boy like Dan and the not-so-young boys, too!

6

October 2, 1852
Early Morning
SOUTHEAST OF CHENEYVILLE, LOUISIANA, ON BAYOU BOEUF

Joseph awakened early, and his stirring caused a chain reaction in the camp. Wood ducks could be heard in the bayou, and the little duckings welcomed the day from a hollow cypress tree trunk. He was intrigued with a lone, green-head mallard that seemed to be looking for his mate. The morning promised good traveling weather, as the blue sky held not a cloud.

The delicious smell of fresh coffee was one of Joseph's favorite smells. They ate their breakfast of biscuits and a little ham left over from the Sunday supper on the grounds, then packed up to move on down the red dirt path.

Before they left, Joseph led them in prayer asking for safety and recited the part of Psalm 91 that says, "He shall give His angels charge over you." He prayed for all his children by name and their families. As they settled in for the morning's ride, Daniel drove the team of horses, and Lemuel sat on the bench in the back beside Dan. Joseph rode semi-reclined, soaking in the beauty all around him.

Joseph noticed that something was bothering young Dan and finally asked, "What's on your mind this morning? Ya got a question for me?"

"Yes, sir, I do. But, I don't want to make you upset or sad."

"Go ahead and ask. There ain't much these days that can pull me down to a frown."

With some hesitation, Dan began. "Great-Grandfather, I noticed that

28

you asked the Lord to bless all seventeen of your children this mornin'. I've heard many times from Father 'bout the other two, but he never gave any details."

The look on Joseph's face changed. He did not respond quickly as he shifted his position on the pallet. Lemuel's expression was even more distraught.

Joseph sighed.

7

June 17, 1830

NEAR OAKDALE, LOUISIANA

ON A VISIT TO JOSEPH'S SON WILLIAM'S HOME

My twin girls, Ruth and Naomi, were absolutely beautiful! Their dark hair framed their little faces in such a way that I 'spect they were prettier than most angels. They were always together, and oh, how they loved to go explorin'. They used to come home with some of the most unusual treasures. As my own father would have said, "They were little ragamuffins." Their mother learned quickly not to dress 'em in pretty, little, girly things, 'cause they'd come home in tatters.

The girls were fidgety and wanted to go out, so Hannah asked William if it was safe for 'em to play outside in the barn. He told her they should be all right. I remember her sayin', "Don't go any farther than the barn, girls."

It was a Thursday mornin', and it looked to be a scorcher. Ruth and Naomi ran off to play in the barn, where it was cooler and they could play in the hay. After about thirty minutes, Hannah noticed she couldn't hear the girls gigglin' in the haystack anymore. We called for 'em, but they didn't answer.

I told Lemuel to go check on 'em. I could hear 'im callin', "Come on out from hidin' and stop playin' 'round. This ain't *no* game, girls! Mother is startin' to git worried." He spent a couple minutes lookin' through the barn. Then we heard 'im holler, "They ain't here!"

Hannah dropped the bowl of beans she'd been snappin' and started runnin' toward the barn. Within seconds, everyone was lookin' in the barn, thinkin' they might have been playin' hide-and-seek.

I went to the open door in the back and looked out. What I saw gave me a cold shiver. There, not but a few feet from the barn door, were some tracks in the dirt. "Look, those are black bear tracks." I knew those woods real good and was well aware of the harm that bears could do. We hadn't heard any noise and no sign of a struggle, so we knew the bear hadn't dragged 'em away, but that didn't mean that the bear wasn't *followin'* 'em.

Hannah cried, "Oh my God!" I knew she was prayin' that the bear wouldn't get to Ruth and Naomi before we did.

All the tracks seemed to be together, so we followed 'em to the edge of woods to a big, ole, hollow log with a few bees buzzin' 'round. That's where the tracks split up. The bear's tracks went one way and the girl's tracks went another, but we lost both sets as the thicker brush covered the tracks. My heart raced! Where were my girls? Where was that bear? Did it coax 'em to follow 'im deeper into the woods?

At the log, I told everyone, "Split up and keep callin' their names." I prayed and tried to remain calm as I pushed through the blackjack, but my mind and heart were racin' mighty fast.

It was Lemuel's voice that brought us all some relief. "They're here! Over here!"

I heard Hannah say, "Oh, Thank God!"

They were lyin' on the ground and tried to get up, but they were stumblin' and staggerin' 'round. The relief I had felt just a few seconds ago turned into a new kind of panic. Neither Naomi nor Ruth was laughin' or gigglin'. I looked carefully at first one and then the other. Their little eyes were filled with fear. Their faces were bright red, and then they both began to vomit. It was a violent kind of sick. We tried to walk 'em back to the house as quickly as we could, but they had to stop every few feet to be sick again. It was Naomi who said, "Can't see very well, Papa. My legs won't work right."

I began prayin', "Lord Jesus, show me what to do. Please, let my babies be all right." I picked up Ruth and told William to carry Naomi.

I yelled back over my shoulder to William, "Have one of your boys go fetch the horse doctor. Tell the doc my girls are in trouble!"

The young Dan stopped his great-grandfather and asked, "Why a horse doctor? Why not a real doctor?"

"Dan, the nearest medical doctor was a hard day's ride away in Alex."

Hannah was already moanin' with fear. We got some blankets and laid 'em on the floor in the dogtrot, where they might catch a little breeze. The sound of their breathin' changed. It seemed raspy—like each breath wasn't enough to sustain 'em.

While Lemuel and William's wife, Rhoda, watched over all the other children, Hannah and I sat with the girls and continued to put cool rags on their foreheads, but it didn't seem to do much good. Their eyes were open, but they were real glassy-lookin'. They kept callin' for us. I still remember their frail little voices. "Mama, where are you?" My heart hurt so to hear 'er say, "Papa, help me!" I knew they were slippin' away from us, and I cried out, "Lord, help 'em."

Hannah and I washed 'em with cool water to bring their fever down. We removed this sticky syrup that stuck to their hands and had dribbled down the front of their shirts. I was positive it smelled like honey, but I thought it strange that our girls were sick from eatin' it.

As time went on, they stopped bein' restless and didn't call for us. The horse doctor only lived a couple miles away, and I could not find it in me to be very patient. I prayed that he was at home and not out at some farm helpin' to deliver a foal.

The most agonizin' hours of our lives were spent in the cool of the dogtrot with our girls. Hannah was tryin' to be strong, but I think we both knew that this was not goin' to end well. We sat and cried quietly, watchin' our precious babies stop strugglin' for air. Within minutes of each other, they went home to be with Jesus.

It just didn't seem right. That very mornin', those six-year-old girls had been full of giggles and joy, and now, seven hours later, they were gone.

Joseph stopped his story and wiped his eyes. "Dan, it just didn't seem fair to have 'em snatched away like that."

The elder Daniel put his hand on Joseph's shoulder and told 'im, "Grandfather, ya don't have to go any further." Joseph glanced up at his grandson with a determined look. "Daniel, I need to finish this story for your sakes—and for mine."

Daniel drew back with tears in his eyes. He had never seen Joseph this emotional, and it gave 'im an uneasy churning in his stomach.

The horse doctor arrived about five o'clock. He went into the dogtrot to find Hannah holdin' the girls on her lap. What happened next was most difficult. The doctor, William, and I had to remove the girls from her grip and carry 'em into a bedroom so he could try to find out what happened. I gently removed their mother from the room. Rhoda tried to comfort my Hannah while the doctor did his work, but she was drownin' in a sea of sorrow. The doctor's arrival had given us just a slight glimmer of hope. But, when he came out, he just shook his head and said, "Pastor, they're gone."

He asked to see the clothin' that they had been wearin'. His next remark surprised me. "I'm no people doctor, but I've seen these symptoms before." He touched the sticky substance and smelled it. "Just as I figured . . . I thought I could smell honey. Bless their little hearts, they ate poisoned honey."

I remember askin' him, "How is that possible? We eat honey often, and no one ever gets sick?"

The doctor pulled a chair out into the dogtrot and sat next to me. We talked for some time. "They probably found a hive that didn't have many bees buzzin' 'round and fooled around long enough to get the comb out without gettin' stung. Problem was, the flowers those bees sucked on for the nectar were poisonous." The doctor shook his head from side to side. "Even if a medical physician lived closer than Alexandria, there is nothin' he could have done to make a difference. There is no cure for honey poisoning. Pastor, don't you worry about any more of the honey. I'll get a group of our friends, and we'll go through the woods and make sure all the hives are destroyed."

I looked into the doctor's eyes. "Why didn't the bear get sick and die? Why my little girls? And where was the Great Physician?"

"Pastor, animals know when nature isn't on their side. Who knows, the bear might have tasted it and gotten sick, but he left *that* honey alone for a reason."

The doctor shook my hand and left. I heard 'im mumble as he headed for his horse, "This poor family . . . so, so sad."

Sad doesn't begin to explain what Hannah and I experienced that day. There was so much that had to be done, ya know, like breakin' the news to the rest of the womenfolk, and then of course—the funeral. My body felt like it weighed five hundred pounds, and I just couldn't seem to move. Hannah wailed and cried uncontrollably as everyone in both families tried to console her. On into the mornin' hours she wept. You remember all this, don't you, Lemuel?

Lemuel wiped his eyes and nodded. "Seems like just yesterday, Father."

"I was so very grateful that William was there to help us through that time. He helped Hannah and me plan out their funeral. We decided that since the girls came into the world together, they should be laid to rest together. The next day, William and the other menfolk worked to build a hand-carved coffin out of a hollow cypress stump. They even made a hand-hewn lid with their names and Matthew 19:14 carved on it.

"Hannah and the other women prepared the girls and dressed 'em in their prettiest matchin' Sunday dresses. I was glad that she showed respect to my mother's Cherokee burial tradition of using oil and lavender on their little bodies. I will never forget that smell.

"We were both beside ourselves with grief, and I really felt the need to get away by myself, so I bridled Ole Sally and didn't even bother to saddle 'er. We followed the trail that led down along the Calcasieu. I slid off her back, dropped to my knees, lifted my hands to heaven, and cried out, 'Why, *why*, Lord, *why?*'"

8

June 27, 1830

CELEBRATING THE LIVES OF RUTH AND NAOMI WILLIS

ON THE BANKS OF THE CALCASIEU RIVER

I want to thank you all for comin' to this spot on the Calcasieu today. The girls would've enjoyed playin' under this flowerin' red buckeye tree. Oh, how they loved flowers. The girls have been in Beulah land for ten days now.

I'm sure many of you are askin' why we buried 'em here and not at the church cemetery. Probably many more of you are wonderin' why their service was not held back in Bayou Chicot at our beloved Calvary Baptist Church.

I have to confess that on that tragic night, I abandoned my wife. I just had to get away by myself so I rode my mule to this very spot. I got off and fell to my knees. I asked the Lord, "Why? I'm seventy-two! Why not take *me*? They had so much life left to live. Haven't I been obedient to Your callin'? Why, *why*, Lord, *why*?"

The silence was deafenin'. Again, I talked to Him, sayin', "I don't understand, but when I get to heaven, it will be the first question I ask You."

It was then that the Lord spoke to my heart. "Joseph, when you get to heaven, you won't need to ask that question. . . . Will you abandon Me now?"

"No, Lord, where would I go? Only You hold the keys to eternal life." I remained quiet for a moment and then spoke to the Lord with the faith of a grain of mustard seed, "Lord, even if You take away the rest of my children, You slay all of 'em today, and take my salvation from me and then cast my soul into hell, I will still praise Your holy name. Lord, I will *never* forsake You. Never, never . . . never again!"

Again, the Lord spoke to my heart, sayin', "Joseph, you are to cross this river into the so-called No-Man's-Land. That's where I'm sending you next."

We chose this place to bury the girls 'cause this is where the Lord has called me to cross another river on this journey called life.

Hannah and me—to honor my mother—cut a piece from the hems of the girls' dresses and replaced 'em with my mother's Cherokee colors from a dress of hers. We have purposed in our hearts to take these pieces of cloth from their dresses 'cross the Calcasieu and bury 'em under that big oak tree you see o'er yonder on the other side.

Joseph, although visibly shaken by his own story, was regaining his strength. He spoke words from his humble but hurting heart. "Boys, I want to tell you that whoever said, 'Time heals all wounds' never lost a child, much less two. We aren't meant to outlive our children."

What most surprised me were three Cherokee who stood near the back of the crowd. They had come across the river from No-Man's-Land. I last saw 'em when I planted Antioch Church over three years ago on the upper reaches of the Calcasieu. I could tell by their faces that they approved of what I did that day.

Joseph sat and shook his head. "Folks came from Alex, Bayou Chicot, Bayou Boeuf, and even from No-Man's-Land and beyond. I'll never quite knew how the news spread so fast and so far. I can tell you that my broken heart began to be sewn back together that day by all the family and friends there, but most of all by the Great Physician.

I told Hannah, "Our girls are with Jesus. Soon, we will see 'em again.

Hannah, sweetheart, we will both see our little darlin's soon. We are but a vapor here on earth." Then I spoke to the crowd: "We wept bitter tears, and I have even grieved in my sleep. I cried so hard that it woke me up. Scripture says that it's all right to grieve, but we're not to grieve as others who have no hope. We have a Blessed Hope. His name is Jesus.

"The Lord called me to cross the Mississippi River, and now He has called me to cross the Calcasieu River. But, there's yet another river we will cross someday soon, called Jordon. We will see our little Naomi and Ruth and the face of our Blessed Hope as we arrive on the other side."

Joseph bowed his head in silence. Lemuel, Daniel, and Dan all felt a sweet peace in that moment. He lovingly looked at each of 'em and continued:

"So many came to the service that they filled up the nearby field. In order for 'em all to hear me, I stood on the back of a wagon and spoke as loudly as I could. But, I know one thing for sure: I shocked 'em that day, and of all things, it was with a bucket. White folks and Cherokee too still talk about it even today.

"As we stood there, I motioned toward a bucket of ashes that sat by the girls' grave. It was hard for everyone to see it 'cause of all the stones piled up. So, I asked for the bucket, and I lifted it high. I felt sort of anxious but also very determined as I explained another Cherokee custom my mother had taught me about mournin' and grief. She had once told me that when a loved one died, the men would put ashes on their heads to show grief and lost love.

"I told 'em, 'No, these are not ashes from William's fireplace. I crossed over the Calcasieu just yesterday and brought back *these* ashes from a fire I made under the oak durin' my time alone with the Lord.' I reached down into that bucket and took some moist ashes and made the sign of the cross on my forehead.

I set the bucket of ashes down. To my surprise, a long line of family and friends lined up for ashes. Not a word was spoken by anyone as we all made the sign of the cross on our foreheads."

9

Late Afternoon, October 1, 1852
HURRICANE CREEK AS IT FLOWS INTO COCODRIE LAKE

For several miles, no one spoke a word in the wagon, for all were lost in thought.

Lemuel watched his father carefully throughout the afternoon as he slept. The bouncy wagon ride would have kept most awake, but then again, most people were not ninety-four. He knew it had to be the hand of the Lord that had kept Joseph alive this long. Lemuel thought, *I'm already forty. Young Dan has already started writin'. I also need to start writin' Father's stories down for my grandchildren. Perhaps someday their grandchildren will write 'em down, too.*

When Joseph finally stirred, his eyes seemed keen and alert as he again started looking for landmarks that indicated their exact location. He immediately recognized where they were as memories flooded his mind. He spoke to Daniel, who was at the reins. "Up here not far is a little veer-off into the woods. Doesn't look like much, but this was one of my favorite fishin' holes. You'll see why when we get there."

Joseph turned and spoke to his great-grandson, "Now, Dan, I know ya asked me yesterday 'bout Mr. Epps and Solomon Northup. What I didn't tell ya was that Epps wasn't Solomon's first owner. He was first owned by a close friend of mine. That's how I became friends and pastor to Solomon."

"What was his name, Great-Grandpa?"

"William Prince Ford."

"You mean *your* friend owned Solomon Northup?

"Yes, but it was before Epps bought 'im. Fact is, William Prince Ford and I used to come to this very spot to fish and talk. He asked me almost as many questions as you do. I knew his father back in South Carolina and have known William since he was a small boy.

❖ ❖ ❖

"When I organized the church near Forest Hill in '41 that you and your father belong to today, Spring Hill Baptist, William Prince Ford was the first church clerk. He would bring Solomon and his other slaves to church with 'im. One of his slaves, Judy, even helped us organize Spring Hill. They made William a deacon the next year, and I ordained 'em in '44 to preach Jesus. The next year, though, in '45, they kicked 'em out of Spring Hill for teachin' the beliefs of Alexander Campbell. Some call 'em Campbellites today.

"Before that happened and he moved away, we'd ride down the banks of Hurricane Creek to this very spot to catch a mess of fish. But, he's still a faithful friend of mine to this very day. Some have a problem with that. I told 'em I can fish with anyone from any church I want, 'cept those that handle 'em snakes. They're welcome to fish with 'em, though."

The bumpy ground jostled them as the elder Daniel followed his grandfather's instructions. Sure enough, Joseph had remembered correctly. He looked a little disappointed as he looked for his landmarks, because it was obvious that others had also discovered his fishing hole by a small child's footprints in the sand. He smiled and said, "Oh, well . . . that's all right.

The woods cleared, and right down next to Hurricane Creek as it flowed into Cocodrie Lake was a perfect place to fish for supper and camp for the night.

"You and Dan can go down and catch some crappie for our supper, and I can sit here and watch from the wagon. What do ya think, sound

41

good? I'm really hungry!"

Within just a few steps, the warm water tickled the shore. "Great-Grandfather, this is gonna be fun! I'm gonna catch me some bream, and we can eat 'em for supper." Dan's face beamed with excitement as he and his father cut a couple cane poles from the banks of the lake. The elder Daniel had brought an axe, a sharp knife, and a loaded gun. The elder Daniel really knew very little about guns, but they all agreed it was wise to bring some form of protection, more than a filletin' knife.

Lemuel unhitched and unharnessed the horses, which he had named Pete and Repete. He took 'em down to the banks of the creek to water 'em. He tied 'em both to a rope, separated 'em, and strung it between two trees. He had brought some oats along for 'em and would tend to 'em while the others fished. While Lemuel waited for the fun to begin, he took the axe and cut some wood for the evening fire. He then set about collecting pine cones and pine straw for kindling. The scent of a pine smoke fire couldn't be matched, in Joseph's mind.

They had the back of the wagon facing the creek so Joseph could enjoy watching them fish. Dan had found some crickets in the tall grass and poked around under an old log for a few worms. It didn't take too long before he had a good strike. It took him a good while to get his fish to the bank, because he had to be careful not to snap his cane pole. He finally pulled out a nice-sized bluegill that fought like a big-mouth bass, in his mind.

Joseph encouraged him the entire time he struggled with what was Jonah's whale to him! "Dan, wear 'im down! Keep playin' with 'im! That's our supper—you can do it!"

Young Dan could hear Joseph laughing with Lemuel in the background. His father had moved out of sight and had no idea about this. When Dan finally got the fish up on dry land, he sat on a rock to calm down.

"Great-Grandfather, my knees feel kind of wobbly! That was fun, but I was 'fraid I'd see moccasins, or even worse, that my fish would get away.

Any gators in there?"

"Dan, don't ya know what Cocodrie means?"

"No sir . . . what, Great-Grandfather?"

"It means *alligator.*"

Dan's jaw dropped. Joseph put his head back and gave a hearty laugh. Dan could not tell if he was laughing at him or if there was something else funny that he had missed, so he politely smiled but remained quiet.

It wasn't but a little while later that Daniel came around the bend in the creek and held up his string of various-sized perch for everyone to see.

Dan announced, "I caught a fish, Father!"

But, before Dan could display his catch, Daniel put his fatherly hand on Dan's shoulder. "Ya only caught *one* fish, Dan? Don't feel bad. Jonah only caught one fish! At least yours isn't big enough to swallow ya."

They all laughed.

Joseph came to young Dan's rescue. "Don't get ahead of yourself, Daniel. Your son did right well. Show 'em, Dan."

Dan held up his one *bigger* fish.

His father's eyes got huge, and he seemed to stumble over his own words. "How'd you catch that? Were you over by some big ole cypress stump? What bait did you use?" He scratched his head and kept looking at that one fish still dangling from the line. "Who helped you?" He glanced at Lemuel for an answer.

Dan looked at Joseph and smiled. "Great-Grandfather guided me with what *he* called 'the Alpha and Omega' of fishin'."

Joseph's smile could not be mistaken as he nodded in agreement. Again, they all laughed.

The elder Daniel looked at the three of them and shrugged. "I've heard that fishin' advice before—a few hundred times. But, that's just like your great-grandfather. He has such an encouragin' way with folks. Always has and always will."

Joseph spoke to Dan. "Son, ya did good. I can remember the first time that your father went fishin'. He didn't catch a single fish for supper that night."

The fish were cleaned and cooked over an open fire, and Dan had never tasted anything quite so good in his entire life.

The fire crackled as the bullfrogs sang their chorus from the edges of the lake. The men could hear an old hoot owl back in the woods. Dan, still being full of energy, caught some fireflies and saved them in a tin can while the men shared good family memories.

At Joseph's insistence, they helped him down out of the wagon, and he joined them at the campfire. One of the small benches from the wagon served as his seat, and he appeared to be comfortable for the time being between the Daniels. Lemuel sat on the other side of the fire.

Joseph said to Dan, "Sure am glad we got this strong breeze tonight to keep the mosquitoes down. I can remember times when the air hung heavy with 'em. In fact, they grew so big that you could saddle 'em and ride 'em. Remember those times, boys?"

Dan smiled, waving his hand in the air, "*Awww*, Great-Grandpa."

Lemuel and Daniel could both recall spending many a night swatting at those pests. Lemuel added, "I don't know which caused us more trouble, the buzzin' around or the bites they gave us."

Dan piled some logs on the fire, and it blazed bright. He sat down close to his great-grandpa this time.

Dan whispered, "Great-Grandpa, I sure do love you."

Joseph whispered back, "I love you, too, Dan."

Dan sat quietly for a moment and then said, "I've got a couple more questions."

"Go ahead, ask away."

"How'd ya meet Miss Elvy, and did ya ever see your friend Mr. Bowie again?"

Lemuel and Daniel snickered a little.

Joseph's response was somewhere between a laugh, a sigh, and surprise at Dan's question about Miss Elvy. "Dan, I'm not sure you're old enough for this story."

"Please, Great-Grandpa, I'm all fetched up! I'm thirteen and a half as of yesterday. I want to hear about Aimuewell and Samuel's mother and how you met her."

"Dan, I need to think about this tonight. Tomorrow, we'll have lots of time to talk at your father's home on Spring Creek. You know, it used to be my ole home place. I built it in 1827 before I moved the family there for good. "

Dan was the last one to go to sleep and the first one to wake up the next morning. They prepared to move out after their breakfast of hard-boiled eggs, and homemade bread with dewberry and mayhaw jelly.

Joseph could tell that Dan was just itching for the story to begin. Daniel and Lemuel were also curious about how he would handle all this.

"Dan, before I tell about Miss Elvy, first things first. I need to help you understand a little more about those years between 1826 and 1833. Now, all this time, I had been travelin' and plantin' churches like Antioch in '26, Amiable in '28, and Occupy Baptist Church in 1833. Hannah, my third wife, got the fever in '31, a year after our girls died, and I took her to the banks of the Calcasieu River to be buried with 'em. I made several more trips into No-Man's-Land when I heard of a settlement down the river that wanted a church. So, I hopped a steamer to see if I could help 'em. When I think back on *that* riverboat trip, I can't help but smile. You asked for it, Dan. . . .

10

April 5, 1833

ALEXANDRIA, LOUISIANA

RIVERBOAT RODOPH ON THE RED RIVER

I wandered around the steamboat Rodoph for a good while after waterin' and feedin' Ole Sally. The good captain had made two exceptions for me that day: he let me bring my mule aboard and agreed to make an unscheduled stop on the banks of the Mississippi to let me off nearer my destination. The captain added that this was his way of havin' a part in the spreading the gospel. He then said, "Perhaps ya could share the Good News with a card sharp that's on board, named George Smith—so he says."

About that time, up walked Mr. Smith. "Sir, my name is George Smith. I hear tell you're some kinda preacher or somethin'. I prefer card-playin' games like vingt-et-un and bettin' pleasures on the horses at Fleetfield Race Track in Natchez. These games are of skill, not chance. So as I see it, it's not a sin, preacher. I'm no card sharp, just a sportin' man tryin' to make a livin'. You agree?"

"Not hardly, but you have a nice day."

The spring weather was pleasant enough that day—not too hot yet, and there was a nice breeze blowin' on the river, and the fog had long since lifted. My thoughts were on visiting Bethel Baptist Church again at Woodville, Mississippi, at the request of Mississippi Governor Abram Scott. I helped establish that church in 1798, and the Governor was now a trustee. He felt concern about the cholera epidemic, the same sickness that took my Hannah, for it was continuing to spread throughout the area and was even thought to be carried by the riverboats. He had asked me to lead a prayer meetin' 'bout the plague. I hesitated to travel by riverboat 'cause of the epidemic, but I had tended to Hannah when she was sick and I didn't catch it, so I wasn't too worried.

It was late mornin', and I was on the far end of the deck when I saw my old friend, Johnson Sweat, and a young female. We greeted each other, and I said, "It's good to see you again. I think the last time we spoke was at your father's school in Bayou Chicot. My children always thought he was a good teacher, and they learned readin', writin' and cipherin' better than I ever did."

Mr. Sweat laughed in agreement. "He had a gift for teachin', and he spoke favorably about your children." He paused and looked back and forth between the young lady and me. "Pastor, I'd like you to meet my daughter, Elvy. Today is her thirty-first birthday, and I promised to take her down the Red River to the Mighty Mississippi on this here river-boat—down to Red Stick, you know. I just love Baton Rouge."

She was ever so polite as she slowly spun her lacey parasol and nodded at me with a slight smile. Her dress was a style I hadn't seen before, for it showed a little more bare shoulder than I was used to seein'. She was very nice. I thought she was a little shy. But, 'cause she knew I was a preacher, she started askin' questions about the Bible.

She glanced at her father with an amusin' sparkle in her eyes and then back at me. "My father says *if* and *when* I get married, I have to be submissive and do what the Bible teaches. What are your thoughts on that, Pastor Willis?"

Boys, I didn't know what kind of answer she was lookin' for, but I knew it wasn't no biblical one, so the best I could do was try to lighten the mood.

Lemuel asked his father, "Did you really tell her one of your jokes?"
Joseph just nodded and said, "'Fraid so."

"Miss Elvy, the way I see it is this: do you remember the story in Genesis of the creation?"

"Yes, Pastor, I do, but not in detail."

"The story goes that Adam told God, 'I want a wife that will cook, clean, help me take care of these animals, and do whatever I tell her to do. How much will that cost me?'

"'An arm and a leg.'

"Adam scratched his head and asked, 'What will a rib get me?'

'Not much!'"

She giggled, but her father laughed right out loud.

I added, "Let me be serious for a moment, Miss Elvy. It does say in Ephesians that a wife should submit to her husband, but it also says in the Bible that they both should submit to each other. In fact, Miss Elvy, it says that a man should be willin' to give his life for his wife, just like Jesus did for His bride. As I figure, it's not a fifty-fifty arrangement as many say today. It's a ninety-ten deal. Each gives ninety percent and expects ten percent in return. If they both do that, then as I see it, they got a good chance of makin' it work. If you meet such a man, then you'll have one worth your interest."

"Oh, my, I never thought of that, Pastor. Is that what you did? You've been married a couple times. Did you and your wives feel that way?"

"When I was married to Rachel, my first wife, we made a decision to get down on our knees every night and pray for each other. You know, Miss Elvy, it's hard to stay angry with someone you're prayin' for."

I studied her face and waited for a response. I realized she was mixed with Indian, too. She had dark eyes and high cheekbones. A different kind of beauty, inside and out.

Dan asked a natural thirteen-year-old's question: "Great-Grandpa, were ya startin' to like 'er?"

"Well, not yet. I thought she was attractive, but she was only thirty-one, and she gave me butterflies 'cause I didn't know what to say to her. It was just too soon to think in that way."

Joseph had a faint smile as he continued his story.

⚜ ⚜ ⚜

It wasn't long after that that Mr. Sweat said, "Pastor, how 'bout supper tonight? It would be enjoyable to sit 'round and hear more of your stories while havin' fellowship at suppertime."

I agreed to meet 'em to eat about 7:00. I watched her gracefully stroll outta sight.

I felt a little undone when she arrived without Mr. Sweat. She walked right up to me and said, "My father has had a flare-up of gout. He's not feeling well enough to join us. I hope you're not too disappointed. My father says I can talk enough for the two of us, anyway."

None of my words seemed to come out right, and I finally told her, "I suppose that would be all right given the situation." For the life of me, I could not figure out why talkin' to her seemed like walkin' with a stone in my boot. It just wasn't comfortable!

She finally started askin' me some questions about our family. Talkin' about that came easy. I talked right up till they brought the pistolettes stuffed with crawfish etoufee and bowls of shrimp and okra gumbo."

Daniel's forehead was all wrinkled up with disbelief. "Grandpa, you actually remember what you ate with her that night?"

"Of course. I remember every detail, 'cause the smell of that Cajun food reminded me of how my Hannah used to cook. She was French, and she knew how to put a smile on my face with her filé gumbo. She could work miracles with a few shrimp, some celery, onions, and peppers. Now, that food on the riverboat did not hold a candle to Hannah's cookin'."

It was Lemuel's turn to ask a question. "Father, you *didn't* mention

Mother that night, did you?"

Joseph laughed and shook his head. "Son, I'm old, but I'm not without feelin's. However, Miss Elvy did."

✤ ✤ ✤

"My father told me about how you lost your wife a while back to cholera. I was so sorry to hear about your loss."

I thanked her, and that's when things got real silent again before she commented, "Pastor, you're more shy than I thought ya would be. You've got plenty years of preaching under your belt, and it seems like the cat's got your tongue. I don't mean to make you uncomfortable."

I was surprised at how brash she was, but she was like a breath of fresh air to me. I found her intriguin'—different, but in a *good* way. With that, she started talkin' and went on for a good long while. She talked 'bout lovin' her books and readin', and how she liked learnin' new things, like how the women in France were taken on more responsibility and becomin' more independent. I just sat there listenin' to her ideas and watchin' her as she shared 'em. I didn't need to say much, but she did have a liberated manner about her. At the end of one of her stories, she stopped, laughed, and apologized for talkin' so much.

"Pastor, tell me about yourself. What do you like to do?"

"Miss Elvy, I like meetin' new people, fishin', studyin', spendin' time with my kids, grandkids, and great-grandkids. And, ridin' through the tall yellow pines on my mule, Ole Sally. And, who knows, I might take a likin' to these riverboat rides someday."

I think we were the last ones to leave the dining area. We stood at the railing and just listened to the bullfrogs on the banks of the roarin' river. The moon was really bright that night, and you could see the cotton and sugarcane fields glistening in its light. An occasional fire dotted the banks, and it was bright enough to see people fishin' for river catfish. The steamer almost had a heartbeat of its own. The steady sound, along with the fresh air, moonlight, and a few lights from the fires, was real peaceful. All of a sudden, down below we heard a whip crack and a cry of pain. I watched her face and saw her wince.

"Pastor, I'd like to get your opinion on that someday."

"Ma'am?"

"Slavery."

"We'll save that for another day."

Her question told me a great deal about her. I felt a need to move her away. "Miss Elvy, I think we have both heard enough. It's gettin' late." She put her hand on my arm, and I walked her to the door. I told her, "Happy birthday. I hope to see you tomorrow before they let me off when we reach the Mississippi."

"I'm sure you will, Pastor Joseph Willis. Lord willin', and the river don't rise." She smiled and disappeared into the room.

I laughed as I made my way back to the main deck. That night, I just sat on a bench for a good long time and wondered, *What just happened?* Ya, know, boys, I almost got the feelin' that Mr. Sweat was playin' matchmaker. By the end of our supper, I had to say it was a memorable night.

"Great-Grandpa, I knew it! You *did* like her after all!"

"Let's just say Mr. Sweat had planted a seed of interest. She was enjoyable to talk with and seemed to have common sense. The thought about our age difference bothered me for her sake, not mine. I knew she was only thirty-one, but I never told her how old I was that night. Come to think of it, I never did tell her my age. She probably figured it out, 'cause she was pretty smart, but she never asked me."

Dan had a big grin on his face. "So, Great-Grandpa, what happened the next day? Did you see 'er before you left the riverboat?"

"Son, glad you asked that. The next day got even better! Her father saw me first thing in the mornin' and almost ran over to me."

✤   ✤   ✤

"My Elvy says that she had a lovely evenin'. I hope she wasn't a pest."

"Good mornin', Mr. Sweat. No, she wasn't a pest. In fact, you've raised quite a lovely daughter."

"Pastor, she can be a handful. I hope she doesn't remain an old maid."

I went on to say, "I did find her to be an interestin' dinin' companion. However, I was truly concerned about your health last night, but it would appear that you are feelin' *much* better today."

"Um . . . you know gout. It comes and it goes. Yes, I am feelin' rather favorable now, thank you. I wanted to invite you to come and visit us the next time you are in the Tenmile Creek area. It's been a little lonely since my wife died. I think Elvy would like that, too. What do you say, Pastor?"

I started to sweat, boys . . . no pun intended! Now, I knew exactly what Mr. Sweat was up to. Part of me wanted to run away like the Joseph in the Bible did. But, another part of me was just a li'l' curious. I saw her comin' across the deck. She looked even prettier than last night, and I think she was wearin' a little rouge, and it wasn't even nighttime. She looked like no *old maid* I'd ever known.

He spoke to Miss Elvy: "I was just askin' the good Pastor to stop by the next time he's in the Tenmile area. Ya know, Elvy, the rumor is that Pastor Willis is thinkin' about startin' a church at Tenmile."

I told 'em, "Mr. Sweat, Miss Elvy, that's no rumor, that's the gospel truth. Fact is, we already bought the land for the church right down on the bank of the creek, and I've already named it Occupy Baptist Church. We still got to clear it, so I will be spendin' a fair amount of time in Tenmile. I certainly hope you will both become members."

"We surely will! We don't have much room, but you're welcome to stay at our humble abode." Miss Elvy seemed charmin' in a mannerly

52

way. She looked right at me and boldly said, I would certainly like it if you would drop by and stay a spell. Who knows, maybe you'll feel more like talking the next time. Ya know, I've been told I make a pretty good huckleberry pie, and a dewberry one, too."

"Oh my. How can I say no to that?"

"I can use an axe, too! I can help you clear a spot for the church."

I just laughed, but her father looked surprised by her comments, because I don't think he'd ever seen her bake a pie, much less use an axe.

I smiled and tipped my hat to her. I had Ole Sally saddled as we approached the Mississippi. I nodded my head and said, "This is where I git off. I'm returnin' to this exact spot in two days to catch this steamer home. Hope to see ya soon."

Little did I know how soon that would be.

"Pastor, that's interestin', because we had originally planned to spend three days but decided to cut our trip short. Never know when my gout might flare up again."

I saw the two of 'em standin' on the deck chattin'. I couldn't help but wonder what they were talkin' 'bout.

Ole Sally and I returned to the banks of the river after we finished our prayer meetin' with Governor Scott about the cholera epidemic. While I was waitin', I cut a cane pole and fished until the riverboat stopped for us. Miss Elvy was on my mind. I wasn't sure whether I should feel excited about the possibility of seein' the Sweats again, or if I should just be still . . . *very still.*

Ole Sally went right up the stage plank with the confidence of a Louisiana politician. I think she enjoyed that riverboat ride, or maybe it was the attention the other passengers gave her, especially the sugarcane the kids offered to her. After we got onboard, I looked around the deck for the Sweats. At first I didn't see 'em, but then they came down the narrow passageway.

We greeted each other warmly and chatted for several minutes, and then I saw a sight I never expected to see. Jim Bowie was walkin' on deck, toting a leather bag. He was wearin' his usual buckskins, and his knife flashed in the sunlight.

"Oh my, excuse me," I said to them. "I see an old friend of mine." Jim must have seen me about the same time, and I went over to 'im. He looked as though he hadn't slept in several days. "Jim, how are ya doin'?"

"Not so good. I was sorry to hear about how you lost your Hannah to cholera. I lost my beloved Ursula to the same deadly scourge. I also lost my two baby angels to the same illness. I heard you lost two youn'uns too. I'm so sorry."

"Pastor, I been wantin' to ask you a question?"

"What's that, Jim?"

"Why did God allow this to happen?"

"Maybe, it will help if I share what I said at my Ruth and Naomi's funeral, but I can't do it right now 'cause I don't want to be rude to my friends. Let's talk about all this later, when we're alone. Come, let me introduce you to my friends.

"Mr. Sweat, Miss Elvy, this is my friend Jim Bowie."

Miss Elvy just stared at him for a moment before she made the comment. "Jim Bowie . . . of the Sandbar fight? Are you really the Bowie who killed a man with your knife after you had been shot and stabbed?"

Jim just smiled and said, "I reckon so ma'am."

We had a little small talk, but I could tell Jim was strugglin' with his feelin', so we excused ourselves and went to check on Ole Sally. After explainin' to Jim the words I spoke at Ruth and Naomi's funeral, it seemed to help 'im. I knew he had been drinkin', 'cause I could smell it on 'im."

"Jim, I really admire you. I've never once heard you use vulgarity or profanity, and you never talk about yourself. I know the pain you feel, 'cause I've been there. But, the bottle is not goin' to solve any of your problems."

"Preacher, I'd rather talk 'bout you. Miss Elvy seems to be nice. But, if you do what I think you're fixin' to do, you're goin' to get all those genteel ladies' tongues a waggin' in your church!"

"That's all right, Jim. Then I'll just have to preach on the meanest member of our church."

"Who might that be?"

"The tongue!"

As I walked away from Jim, I said a silent prayer. "Lord, am I wrong to pursue this?"

❖   ❖   ❖

Joseph had a smile that none of the boys could read. He asked 'em to stop so he could stretch a bit. Young Dan seemed almost impatient with the stop, which took a good while.

After they got started again, he finally asked, "Did Mr. Bowie ever tell you what he was doing on the riverboat, Great-Grandpa?"

"No, and I didn't ask, but I 'spect it had somethin' to do with slaves down in N'Orleans."

❖   ❖   ❖

That night, we went to supper together, and this time everyone was there. They were all curious about Jim. Both asked all sort of questions— especially Miss Elvy.

We ate catfish pan-fried with a cornmeal batter, just like I like it. I wish I had some right now. About halfway through our meal, the captain came to our table and said, "Don't let me interrupt you, but I finally figured a way to serve the Lord. I will make special stops for preachers that are spreadin' the gospel. Ya know, folks, we never do this for anybody, but Pastor Willis gave me the idea when he asked me to do it for 'im. I presented it to the steamline, and to my surprise they said yes. Because of you, Pastor, we're pickin' up another preacher just 'round the bend. You might even know 'im."

"Captain, what's his name?"

"His name is Reverend Murrell. John Murrell."

Jim and I stared at each other in utter silence. We were both speechless. A cold chill went up my spine.

"Great-Grandpa, what did Mr. Murrell do when he saw you and Mr. Bowie?"

"We didn't see each other that night, but the next day, oh my. Let me tell ya what happened."

11

April 9, 1833
RIVERBOAT RODOPH
ON THE RED RIVER

I woke up late and almost missed breakfast. There wasn't much left, but I did get a couple of beignets and some steamin'-hot French roast coffee. I did not see any of my friends, so I just sat quietly and enjoyed the ride.

Most everybody had left the dining area, and as I was gettin' up to leave, John Murrell walked in all by himself. When he finally saw me, the look on his face made my blood run cold. He walked right up to me and shoved me back against the wall. He pinned my shoulders there against the rough wood and just stared at me. His face was ever so red! Quiet, angry words came out of his mouth. His face was just inches from mine, and all I could see was the hate in his eyes. His breath was as hard as kerosene.

"Preacher, it's been a long time, but I've never forgotten what you and your friend Bowie did to me back in 1810. Do you remember?" He was so angry he was spittin' his words. "Let me tell you, in case your ole memory has gotten foggy! You embarrassed me in front of all my friends. You accused me of stealin' horses from a meetin' where I had just shared the gospel. I was just plunderin' hell and populating heaven, and you erroneously blamed me for stealin' from the flock! Your friend Bowie got the jump on me, put a knife to my throat and made me apologize. I still have the scar where his impatience cost me a little bit of my blood. Do you remember that?"

"Yes, I certainly do recall how you preached a sermon and ended it by tellin' 'em to sing a couple of hymns . . . I was there that night. Did you know I went just to hear you? I had to minister to those folks after they went out to find you had plundered their horses and mules. What *you* did was wrong. You stole from 'em."

He moved in closer. "No, what you did was wrong. You humiliated me in front of my friends . . . and strangers. But, your friend with the Arkansas toothpick is not here to protect you now."

I did not speak a word.

"You know what, preacher man, today is your lucky day. You're fixin' to feed thousands today like Jesus did. Yup, you are going to the bottom of this muddy river, where you'll feed thousands of crayfish, catfish, and gators. I'm fixin' to even make you more holy!"

With that, he pulled out his gun and waved the fancy pistol in my face.

Before we got to the door, I started to pray. "Lord, I need some help here."

All of sudden, from behind came a *swoosh* and a loud *thump*. A knife had grazed Murrell's hand and stuck in the wall about three inches from my head. Murrell screamed in pain. Jim Bowie was all over him like white on rice.

Murrell dropped his gun, and Jim kicked it away. He quickly pulled his knife back out of the wall, releasing Murrell's hand. Murrell clutched his bloodied hand in agony. "Look what you've done to me!"

"It's not half of what I'm about to do. You were right about somebody goin' for a swim today, but you had the wrong person. Your blood in the water should attract you a big congregation today." Murrell protested, "No! No, you can't do this. I don't swim real good."

"That's not my problem." Jim pushed 'im to the railing.

I told Jim, "Don't kill 'im. Let him live."

"Pastor, I have no intention of killin' 'im this time. But, by the end of today, he might wish he was dead, though."

The look on Murrell's face was no longer hateful. He was scared! He was beggin' for mercy. I think Jim gave him grace by not killin' 'im when he had the chance.

At the railin', Jim and I looked at each other, shrugged, and then Jim pushed Murrell overboard.

You could hear his cuss words and then a big splash. He yelled up at us, "Hey, what about my clothes and my money? I need 'em!"

"So do the good folks you stole from," I said. "We'll make sure to give your clothes to the poor and to buy a couple horses to replace the ones you stole."

He was still yellin' like a cat on a hot tin roof when the riverboat moved outta hearin' range. We just stood there and watched 'im tryin' to swim to the banks of the river. Good news for 'im was that this happened in a narrow spot in the river, so I was sure he'd make it.

Jim and I just stood there watchin' as the riverboat wake bobbed 'im up and down in the water like a cork. I had to ask 'im, "Jim, how'd ya know you were gonna hit Murrell with the knife and not me?"

"I didn't, Pastor! I just trusted your Lord to protect ya."

Jim continued smiling. Me, not so much.

We walked back into the dining area to retrieve that nice pistol. Jim picked it up and looked at it carefully. "This is a Denix pistol. I think it's Italian made. Ain't seen one in real life, but I've heard tell of 'em. What a beauty. Has to be all of fifteen inches long, and look at all that ornate carving on it. Wonder where he got this?" Jim just shook his head as he looked at me. "Never mind, I think we both know the answer to that." He gripped the gun easily and said, "Ya know, Pastor, I think I might just keep this one. The Lord's people will have no need of it."

About that time, Miss Elvy came into the dining area. "Good mornin', gentlemen. What have you two been up to today? Anything exciting?"

Jim carefully slipped the pistol out of sight as I responded. "Oh, nothin' . . . just the usual . . . for us, that is."

"Oh, I hoped I was gonna get to see somethin' thrillin' today."

We both shook our heads.

❧   ❧   ❧

"Great-Grandpa, did you ever tell her?"

"Tell her what, son?"

"About Mr. Bowie throwin' the devil preacher in the Red River?"

"No, son. Discretion is the better part of valor. And I did not wish to brag. After Jim discretely disposed of the weapon, he returned, and we spent some pleasant time with Miss Elvy. I could tell by Jim's conversation that he approved of her, and it meant a lot to me. She finally excused herself, but before she left, we made plans to meet later in the afternoon. Jim and I had several hours just to sit and talk."

"Great-Grandpa, did Mr. Bowie say anythin' about Texas?"

"Strange that you should mention that, Dan, because that's all he *would* talk 'bout! He talked about a great man he'd met, and from what I've known of 'im over the years, Steven F. Austin was truly a man of vision. That's how he got the name 'Father of Texas.'"

"Great-Grandpa, I wanna hear what Mr. Bowie said about Texas. Ya know, I'm gonna go there someday, too. And maybe buy some of 'em Texas Longhorns."

"Jim couldn't say enough about his beloved Texas and liberty and freedom. Oh, how it reminded me of when I was his age, fightin' with the Swamp Fox for independence from tyranny."

12

December 23, 1833

"Pastor, I wanna tell ya 'bout *Coahuila y Tejas*."

"Go ahead, Jim, tell me." His face shone with a deep passion, almost like he was speakin' of a beautiful woman.

"As far as you can see in every direction, there is beauty. This woman that I call *Liberty* has great dreams, visions, and righteous indignation 'bout what's been happenin' to her people, and a keen sense of right and wrong. All she wants is justice, freedom, and safety for her children." I did not respond but sat there and just listened.

"In this glorious land known as *Coahuila y Tejas*, the rivers carry our dreams, the deer and antelope are bigger, and the music is sweeter. There is a stirrin' for something bigger, and better in the hearts of its people. The people are friendlier, but fiercely loyal to help her stand and take her first steps toward freedom. *Tejas* is my home, the place my two children were born, where I married Maria Ursula, where they're all buried now. No one is driving me off my land without a fight.

"Ya know, I moved there in 1830 and swore my allegiance to Mexico before I married Maria Ursula Veramendi that next year. Pastor, she was such a good wife, and I loved her. Still do." Jim just shook his head. "I don't think I have very good luck with the women. I lost my Cecelia just two weeks before we were to be married by you, and now this."

"Jim, I don't have the words."

"Let me tell you what's put a burr under my saddle blanket! It's so hard to watch the politics—the deceit and greed that causes some Mexican politicians to do such unthinkable acts. There are new, unfair laws every time we turn around, and they make life unbearable. There are many who have caught this dream and can't let it go. We are willin' to fight to the death for independence from these tyrants. Let me tell you some of the things that have happened.

"I met this man, Sam Houston. Pastor, you'd really like him. You and Houston have a lot in common."

"Like what, Jim?"

"Your mother's people, the Cherokee, call him *Colonneh*."

He caught me off guard. "That's Cherokee for *raven*. How did he get that name?"

"He lived with the Cherokee for several years and was adopted by 'em. He even married a Cherokee like your pa did. He lived with a tribe led by Ahuludegi, and I have even heard Houston speak Cherokee. The very same things your mother taught you about others—givin' freely, being brave and speaking honest words—reminds me of Houston's words. While *these* Cherokee are not slaves like you were, Pastor, they are still being treated terribly. I know it caused Houston grief when his friend, Andrew Jackson, decreed that the Cherokee would be driven off their own land. Thankfully, some of 'em have been able to jump off the steamboats before they got 'em to what the Choctaw call *okla humma* and made their way to the refuge of No-Man's-Land.

"When Houston left Washington, he was sick of the evils of government there and went on to *East Texas*, but it didn't take 'im long to get involved in politics again. Like it was for you, Pastor, in the American Revolution, that same passion is stirrin' in the hearts of many in *Tejas* for independence."

"How did you come to know Sam Houston?"

Jim responded, "We got to know each other well during thirteen days back in April of this year when we were both representatives at San Felipe de Austin at a convention. We drafted a list of our grievances to be delivered to the Mexican government. Pastor, I'm not alone in my love for this vast land.

"I gave a letter of introduction to Stephen F. Austin from one of his father's original three hundred colonists. Now, Austin is another man you'd admire. We immediately took a likin' to each other because of our dreams for the future of *Tejas*.

"The Mexican people are gracious folks, like my late wife and her family. But, I have an issue with two Mexican scoundrels. One is Antonio López de Santa Anna. He was elected president of Mexico this year, and I think he is a dangerous man. He does not tell the truth. Santa Anna is to be watched. Mark my words, Pastor, he is going to cause trouble for *Tejas*.

"The other one is a *loco* Mexican army commander named José de las Piedras. He follows Santa Anna's orders. He demanded that everyone in Nacogdoches surrender their weapons. You can imagine how well that went over with me!" Jim and I both laughed. "I was in Natchez when I heard about it and quickly went back home to *Tejas*.

"Stephen F. Austin asked me to see if I could help resolve this issue without bloodshed. In August of last year, several of us marched into Nacogdoches to present our demands to Piedras. Before we reached the officials' offices, we were attacked by about one hundred men with the Mexican cavalry. We returned fire in this fierce battle. It has sparked a wildfire for independence.

"Ya'll know, it is an honor to stand with men like Houston and Austin. They are both noble men, and I 'spect someday people are gonna remember their names."

I added, "Jim, that could be said of you, too!"

"Pastor, I know all about the work you're doin', but I also know they need churches in *Tejas*, too. Why don't you come back to with me? I've got to get back to my home in San Antonio de Béxar, and I know that things are fixin' to change.

"My late father-in-law's home was near *Mission San José*. My Maria

Ursula loved it there, and she would say, 'It's a shame that we don't have more missions like Mission San José and like *Mission San Antonio de Valero, the Alamo* used to be, before Mexican soldiers made it into a fort.' Pastor, there's another reason you need to go with me to *Tejas.*"

"I'll give it some thought, Joseph answered. "I have been in Louisiana for over thirty years, and I'm just not sure that my work here is finished."

"Pastor, I understand." He was quiet for a moment and then added, "Who's to know what'll happen? Santa Anna might even cross the Sabine and make his way to your beloved Calcasieu River. I heard he had even once thought of invading Cuba."

❧ ❧ ❧

Joseph spoke to Lemuel, Daniel and Dan with intensity. "I almost think I hurt his feelin's when I didn't immediately agree to go west with 'im. He had such a burnin' passion for Tejas's future and freedom." He lived only a few days after his beloved Tejas became the Republic of Texas. I wish he would have lived to see it become the state of Texas.

Young Dan asked, "Did you ever see Mr. Bowie after that day?"

"No, son, sure didn't. But, I sure miss 'im. We were opposites in about every way, but I respected 'im as a man. As I said earlier, Jim never spoke about himself. He also never used vulgarity or profanity. I liked 'im and trusted 'im more than many church folk I know.

"Jim agreed to lead his volunteers to defend the Alamo against Santa Anna. He was supposed to get everyone out and destroy the fort but did not have the oxen or horses needed to move the heavy artillery, and there was very little ammunition, I'm told. That's the story that's been handed down, but I've often wondered if the real reason that he volunteered in the first place and didn't want to leave once he got there was because it was his home. His beloved wife grew up near Mission San José. He married her there, his children were born there, and he converted to the Catholic faith there. Knowin' Jim as I did—he wasn't leaving. Can you blame 'em? From what I've heard, Jim was sicker than a dog most of those thirteen days that they stood against the forces of evil.

"Boys, my heart hurt when I heard the news in 1836, but I also know that he died defendin' freedom. Jim Bowie and those other brave men were willin' to lay down their lives. That is exactly what happened at the Alamo. The Good Book says, 'There is no greater love than a man lay down his life for a friend.' That's what they did at the little mission fort. Son, as I see this woman that Jim called Liberty, I can understand their passion for this lone star called Texas today which shines so bright. It's men and women like Jim Bowie that make it shine so bright, even today."

The elder Daniel asked his grandfather, "Did you ever *really* consider followin' Mr. Bowie to Texas?"

"Yes, I sure did, and I almost made it there."

13

October 3, 1852

NEAR BABB'S BRIDGE, LOUISIANA

ON SPRING CREEK

Joseph appeared lost in his memory as the team of horses followed the banks of Cocodrie Lake, headed due west.

Young Dan watched his great-grandfather carefully and finally spoke. "You've told me so much about your life, but do you mind if I ask more questions?"

"I thought you might. Go ahead and ask 'em."

"Grandpa, I have a few questions of my own." Daniel was nodding his head.

Lemuel chimed in, "Me, too, Father!"

Joseph just grinned and said, "We have a few more miles to go, so maybe I can help ya make sense of things before we get to your home, Daniel. Dan, what did you want to ask?"

"You told us you *almost* went to Texas. Why didn't you?"

"I had decided I wanted to see Texas, plant a church or two, and maybe even find Jim. I felt excited about the idea of headin' farther west. I saddled Ole Sally, loaded my packhorse, and headed west to the Sabine River. The closer I got to Burr's Ferry, the less sure I was about my decision. I got right up to the river's edge and was gettin' ready to pay my toll when I got this real uneasy feelin'. As clear as I'm talkin' to you boys, I heard the Lord tellin' me, 'This is not what I've called you to do.'

"At that moment, I knew I had made a terrible mistake. I had made my own plans without askin' the Lord. Ole Sally, my packhorse, and I turned back, and I'm certainly glad we did.

"Ya know the story goes that John Murrell, the devil preacher, buried his loot in some caves not far from there. Who knows, maybe there are a few gold pocket watches there that he stole from my friends, but that was not my concern that day." Joseph smiled.

"Great-Grandpa, did he ever get caught?"

"Yes, Dan, if I rightly remember, he went to prison for ten years, and I heard that he died soon after leavin' prison. Now, Daniel, did you have a question for me?"

"Grandpa, when ya headed back, did ya see Miss Elvy again?"

⚜ ⚜ ⚜

"I surely did! It was on my way back, after I stopped at a café in Natchitoches. I was havin' some supper and struck up a conversation with a man named Jean Baptiste Louis Metoyer. He was buyin' lumber to build a new plantation house, and when he noticed I was dark-skinned he told me how his grandmother, Marie Thérèse Coincoin, had once been a slave. Her generous master of nineteen years gave her and her children their freedom. He even left his plantation to her. Jean Baptiste told me stories 'bout growin' up and havin' slaves waitin' on 'im. He invited me to come visit 'im at his thrivin' Melrose Plantation. I did so on one of my trips to Natchitoches, and he showed me some great hospitality. What a grand place it is along the Cane River. We became good friends.

"When I went back to pastor Occupy Baptist Church, I visited Miss Elvy. She attended Occupy, and we got to know each other much better. Boys, she never wanted me to go to Texas, so she was very glad when I told her my plans had changed. We spent many hours sittin' and talkin' on the courtin' couch in Mr. Sweat's parlor. It was in early May of '34 when I asked Mr. Sweat for her hand in marriage. Now, I know the age difference was a problem for her, because she used to tell me how her brothers teased her. If they weren't calling her an *old maid*, they were laughin' at her for being too young for me. When we finally got engaged, the teasing stopped. Miss Elvy was a headstrong young woman and still is.

"I was grateful to have so many family members and friends there at our wedding in late June of '34. She was a beautiful bride in her white dress, and with those dark eyes and long black hair all the way down to her waist. I can remember her talkin' 'bout havin' an instant family and how happy she was to be surrounded, loved, and accepted by all of you. We settled into marriage quickly, and I continued workin' with Occupy Church."

Lemuel asked, "What was it like in No-Man's-Land back then?"

"Oh my son! You'll have to imagine a place where there was no law and no one to enforce a law if there had been any. In those days, it was a vast land strechin' all the way to the Sabine and claimed by no nation. In No-Man's-Land at that time, there were outlaws, pirates, counterfeiters, runaway slaves, and fugitives from the law. There were tribes like the Choctaw and others who lived peaceably. There were also the Cherokee Jim spoke of, those who had escaped off the steamboats headed up the Mississippi to take 'em away from their native lands to reservations. I made a point of becomin' friends with many of these tribes, especially my mother's and my people, the Cherokee.

"I tried to minister to as many of the outlaws, runaway slaves, fugitives, and others as best I could. Fed and clothed 'em when they were in need, and shared the gospel when they'd listen. I baptized many an Indian and fugitive from who knows where in those days. Many memories flood my mind, like once when I was on a trip up on the Ouachita River. I met a Choctaw man who was very sick, along with his wife, Ohoyo. I prayed for 'em and was able to hunt for some game for 'em. They both went on the mend. What a blessin' that was to me.

"They were the last, the least, and the lost in that hostile land—exactly the kind of folks the good Lord had called me to. I loved it. They were sorta like the Samaritans that were despised in the Bible.

"Some were dangerous men. However, there were many others who were not that and had grown up there. They called it *home*. Not everyone who lived there was a fugitive. Some were doin' their very best to survive, like Miss Elvy and 'er family.

"She grew up there. Bein' mixed with Choctaw, she was accepted and got along well with those who had escaped from the Trail of Tears. My Cherokee roots helped me aplenty as I preached in that lawless land.

"Years before, there was another place that was just as dangerous as No-Man's-Land that I dared to venture into the Louisiana Territory. It was in March of 1800, down in Vermilionville, and the law of the land was the Spanish Black Code. It forbade any preachin' other than Catholicism. They came after me in the middle of the night. A friend of mine, Jacques Cormier, caught wind of the mob's plans and warned me. They were goin' to sell me to the silver mines in Mexico, or even worse, *kill me*. I fled so fast that I didn't have time to put on my boots. That's when they started callin' me the 'Barefoot Preacher' and the Apostle to the Opelousas."

Everyone listening to Joseph's account laughed as he continued.

❖   ❖   ❖

The good Lord has saved me from many dangers. Once, when I was travelin' through No-Man's-Land, I stopped at an inn for the night. Inside, there was a man burnin' up with fever. I asked 'im, "What's your name?"

"Malachi, Malachi Perkins . . . from Tenmile Creek," he replied.

"Do you know Jesus?"

"Yes, sir, I do!" Malachi affirmed.

"That's good!" I wasn't sure he would live through the night, but I fed 'im, brought 'im cool water, and prayed with 'im. That night, I slept like a baby till I heard a faint knock at my door. When I opened it, there he stood, leanin' against the door frame, sweatin' with his fever. "You have to leave. I heard three men talkin' about robbin' and killin' you. They think you have money. I know of a lesser-known trail you can take to safety.

I dressed quickly, and this time I put on my boots and went out the window. I saddled Ole Sally in the barn next to the inn, and off we went in the early hours of the mornin'. She could run like a deer back then. Thank God for a full moon, for I found the path he was talkin' about and got away without any trouble. It kind of reminded me of the story of how the angel came to Joseph and told 'im to take Mary and baby Jesus and flee into Egypt. This was not the first time, nor would it be the last, that the Lord sent a messenger to warn me of danger.

✤ ✤ ✤

Young Dan asked another question. "Great-Grandpa, why did Uncle Lemuel send a hospital wagon to bring you to live with his family? I've asked 'im, and he would never say. Why aren't you still livin' with Miss Elvy?"

The elder Daniel spoke up. "Dan, you don't ask your great-grandpa personal questions like that."

The silence felt uncomfortable. "It's a reasonable question, Daniel. I don't mind if he knows. Dan, I understand why you're askin'." Joseph nodded, then noticed Daniel and Lemuel's eyes were open—wide. They could not believe that Dan had asked the question or much less that Joseph was going to answer it.

"You see, when I married Miss Elvy, she was only thirty-one, and I was seventy-something. She was a wife like the woman described in Proverbs 31, and as you know, she blessed me with two more sons, Samuel in '36 and Aimuewell in '37. We had many happy years together. But, as I grew older and needed more help, she just couldn't take care of me. I think it got to be too much for her. She sometimes sounded so tired and frustrated that it made me feel sad for her.

"Out of her exhaustion, she began to speak unkind words. I know those were not her true feelin's, but she was just so weary. When Lemuel and his family came to visit a few months back, I told 'im that I was makin'

70

her unhappy. I did not want to be a burden to her. I can't blame Miss Elvy. I still love her, and I know she still loves me too. Now, it's my turn to ask a question." Everyone looked rather surprised as Joseph changed the subject. "Dan, there is something I've been meanin' to ask you since we left Evergreen."

"Yes, sir."

"What are ya gonna do with Jesus?"

"Sir, I don't understand."

"Jesus hung between two thieves on a cross. One of 'em rejected Him that day, but the other one asked Him, 'Will You remember me when You enter Your kingdom?' Now, Dan, both of those men were guilty. One said yes to Jesus, and the other said no. One put his trust in Jesus, and the other chose not to. The question is, which thief on the cross are you?"

"Great-Grandpa, I want to be like the one who said yes."

"Dan, there's a Scripture that I love, and it explains things so simply that even I can understand. It says, 'If thou shalt confess with thy mouth the Lord Jesus, and shalt believe in thine heart that God hath raised him from the dead, thou shalt be saved. For with the heart man believeth unto righteousness; and with the mouth confession is made unto salvation.' Dan, you can settle this question right now in heaven and on earth."

"Sir?"

"By sayin' yes to Jesus, just as that one thief did on the cross. It's just as this old Cherokee slave that you call Great-Grandpa once did, too."

"Yes, sir, I want to do that. But, how?"

"I'll tell ya how I did it as a young boy 'bout your age."

"How was that?"

"I just said a prayer to the Lord. There are no exact words. And prayin' is just talkin' to the Lord."

"Will you help me do that, Great-Grandpa?"

"I sure will. I'll pray, and if these words are how you feel in your heart, you can repeat 'em. "Heavenly Father . . ." Dan began to pray too. "I come to You in prayer, askin' for the forgiveness of my sins. I confess with my mouth and believe with my heart that Jesus is Your Son, And that He died on the cross at Calvary that I might be forgiven. Father, I believe that Jesus rose from the dead, and I ask You right now to come into my life and be my personal Lord and Savior. I repent of my sins and will worship You all the days of my life. Because Your word is truth, I confess with my mouth that I am born again and cleansed by the blood of Jesus! In Jesus' Name I pray. Amen!"

"I do believe that in my heart, Great-Grandpa."

"Praise the Lord, Dan! Ya know, after *I* made my decision, I got myself baptized."

"Why?"

"Because the Lord said to."

"Great-Grandpa, I want to do that, too!"

"We're 'bout a mile from your home on Spring Creek, and that'll be a good place to get baptized. The other wagons should already be there from Evergreen."

The elder Daniel looked puzzled. "Grandpa, are *you* gonna baptize 'im?"

"No, Daniel, I think you should. The strength has mostly gone from this temporary home."

"Dan, I'm sure your mama and sisters and brothers will want to witness this glorious occasion."

Joseph smiled and spoke quietly under his breath, "Lord, who is likened unto You?" This was a day that all would remember in the Willis family.

Dan leaned in close to his great-grandfather and gave 'im a big hug. He whispered in his ear, "I sure do love you, Great-Grandpa . . . and my Jesus, too."

Lemuel reined the team of horses 'round the bend. "We'll be at Daniel's home shortly."

Joseph was grateful, because his bones were sore from being jostled for three days. When they pulled up, everyone came out to greet them. It was a joyous reunion, especially when they took young Dan down to Spring Creek to be baptized. Lemuel and Daniel carried Joseph down the path to the creek. Dan and his father stepped into the cold creek, and when young Dan came up out of the water shivering, he had the biggest smile his family had ever seen!

Dan walked right up to his great-grandfather. "Great-Grandpa, what do I do now?"

"I'll give you two words of advice my mother gave me many times. She would say, 'Son, the only Bible that most people ever read is our lives.' And Dan, every time I went to her for advice, her answer was always the same: 'Joseph, what would Jesus do?' Write those two down in your tablet son, and write them on the tablet of your heart, too. Pray and trust Him at all times, and study God's Word, and count your blessin's daily. And, Dan, remember that it's what you sow that multiplies, not what you keep in barn."

As they carried Joseph back to the house, he could smell a savory stew. The fragrance of fresh bread filled the air, and Joseph's stomach growled. When he was settled, they brought him a bowl of piping-hot venison stew. He gave thanks and ate slowly, enjoying every single bite. He also gave thanks for finally having a soft chair to sit in.

Dan brought his plate of food over closer to his great-grandfather so he could sit and talk. Joseph could see that something was troubling him. "You look like something's on your mind. Let's hear it."

Everyone stopped eating to hear Dan's question. "Will ya tell me about Mr. Ford's slave, Solomon Northup?"

"I'll do that, but I first need to get some rest and read the Word. We can talk about it in the mornin.'"

Joseph had a peaceful rest that night. He awoke the next mornin' at the break of dawn with the sound of an old rooster crowing and the smell of Louisiana dark roast coffee and biscuits baking in a cast-iron skillet.

Daniel's wife, Anna, had cooked a hearty breakfast of fried eggs, ham, and biscuits with gravy, and there were mayhaw and dewberry jellies, too. After Joseph got cleaned up, they carried him out and placed him gently in a chair at the head of the table. Young Dan took a seat right next to him.

Joseph had hardly given thanks and swallowed his first bite when Dan asked, "Are you ready to tell us about Mr. Ford and Solomon Northup?"

"Yes, Dan, I am, but first let me tell you what led up to me meetin' Solomon Northup. I hope you're ready to hear all this."

14

What a memorable day Sunday, August 8, 1841, turned out to be! That was the day I founded Spring Hill Baptist Church. It was the last church I ever organized. All sixteen organizing members were present, including William Prince Ford, and Judy, a slave woman of color owned by William. William brought all his slaves that day, including two newly bought ones whom I did not recognize. There was standin' room only, and it was a scorcher! Many of the plantation owners and their slaves were there, too. My heart was full of joy. P.W. Robert, Robert Tanner, and William Prince Ford each stood and spoke encouragin' words 'bout the new church. They had asked me to come and deliver the message that morning, and I'd gladly accepted. I spoke to 'em about makin' good choices. I told 'em what my mother always taught me to ask when makin' a decision: 'What would Jesus do?'

Truth is, a new church always faces adversities in the early days—if not all of its days. There were plenty of "amens" and noddin' heads as the hand fans fluttered. We sang a couple of my favorite hymns, "Amazing Grace" and "Rock of Ages."

"After church, William Prince Ford asked to make an announcement. He declared, 'I'd like to say a few words. This is a great day for our community. My wife, Martha, and I were plannin' on having a small celebration at our plantation this afternoon, bHurricaut after talkin' to Pastor Willis, we want to make it very special and invite everyone in our community. At

Pastor Willis' request, we are goin' to make it a celebration of thanksgivin'.

"So, next Saturday, we're havin' some of the best eatin' this parish has ever seen, with music and games for the kids too—young and not so young. Did I mention the hayrides and a horse race or two? Also, Daniel Willis wants to organize a new game from up North called baseball. He explained it to me. It will never catch on, but you can sign up with 'im.

"Ladies, please bring your favorite covered dishes! I'm thinkin' we'll have plenty of corn on the cob, potatoes, fresh produce from your gardens, and of course, some mouth-waterin' desserts. We're gonna have fresh-smoked hams from my new smokehouse. And, we're also gonna serve up a couple dozen smoked turkeys, a side of beef cooked over an open fire, and with any luck we'll have some fresh venison." William looked at a couple of the best local hunters and grinned. "And that's what Martha came up with in the last ten minutes." Everyone laughed and clapped, and the plannin' for the celebration of thanksgivin' was underway.

I couldn't recall anything like that ever happenin' 'round here. It reminded me of a celebration my late wife Rachel would often speak of that was handed down through her ancestor, William Bradford. People were gettin' excited just thinkin' 'bout a day of thanksgivin', fellowship, fun, and Southern recipes. That week passed quickly, and everywhere we went, people were talkin' 'bout it. Now, Dan, to answer your question about Mr. Ford's slave, Solomon Northup. . . .

15

August 14, 1841

WILLIAM PRINCE FORD WALLFIELD PLANTATION
ON HURRICANE CREEK NEAR FOREST HILL, LOUISIANA
FEAST OF THANKSGIVING CELEBRATION

When we arrived late Saturday mornin' at the Fords' Wallfield plantation, there were so many people there was no way to count 'em all. Everybody was enjoyin' the unseasonable fall-like weather. A gentle, cool breeze off Hurricane Creek and a few clouds kept the normally stiflin' heat down. Several small groups of men gathered to talk politics, who had the fastest horse, and of course, the weather. The womenfolk were busy cookin' in the log kitchen, gettin' the food in order, takin' care of the babies, and watchin' the toddlers. The conversations were as lively as the toddlers.

The older children were down in the field, competin' in sack races and swingin' off a rope into the creek's swimmin' hole. The younger girls played hopscotch and pick up sticks, and there were dolls everywhere. It had all the makin's of an unforgettable day.

We made our rounds, greetin' old friends and meetin' new ones. There were people from Cheneyville, Bayou Chicot, Bayou Boeuf, Alex, No-Man's-Land, and as far away as N'Orleans. Some of the plantation owners' wives wore the newest fashions, like William Prince Ford's wife, Martha Tanner Ford. She looked like she had been shoppin' in N'Orleans's finest stores. And Madam Mary McCoy, the beloved angel of mercy from Norwood Plantation, walked around in finery rumored to be from Paris and greeted all the guests, including the slaves. Madam McCoy was known for the Christmas parties she provided for the slaves down Bayou Boeuf way. Miss Elvy, in her crisp, blue gingham dress, chose to stay with the women and children, and I excused myself to talk with several of the men. The savory smell of the meats smokin' gave us a growin' appetite. There was an abundance of food and, Dan, it all looked good!

I noticed a slave fiddler playin' a happy jig, "Skip to My Lou," while the children danced around 'im. He strolled around and smiled as he played requests. I recognized 'im from church the week before. He seemed to hang on my every word. I watched 'im carefully and thought, *I wonder how a slave learned to play like that*! When I finally found William, I asked 'im about his musician.

"That fiddler is pretty good, isn't he?" he said. "His name is Platt, and he belongs to me. I bought 'im down in N'Orleans a few weeks back. He works at my lumber mill up on Indian Creek. Seems to be a good worker so far, and . . . well, he's lots smarter than most."

Dan, I remember this clearly. Platt started playin' a song called "Sweet Canaan," and a woman's angelic voice began singin' from 'er heart. All eyes and ears were on 'em with their pleasin' music. When they finished, everyone clapped for 'em, and they both took a bow. I found out later that this song about leavin' for heaven had an additional meanin' 'bout slavery.

Then smiling at him I said, "William, I sure would like to hear 'im play another tune or two, maybe even a Negro spiritual, if he is able. I really love those songs. Mind if I ask 'im?"

"No, Pastor, go right ahead. I reckon he can play 'bout anything by ear. However, we do need to get people to the tables so we can eat before the food gets cold."

William rang the bell that was mounted on a pillar on the porch, and everyone found a seat. He asked me to say the blessin'.

"Friends, before I say the prayer, I want to tell you 'bout another feast of thanksgivin'. I remember hearin' my late wife Rachel talk about the harvest feast back in the days of the Pilgrim leader, William Bradford.

He was her ancestor. He traveled to this New World in 1620 on the Mayflower to seek religious freedom. They were not prepared for what they found, and had it not been for the kindness and generosity of the Indians livin' up there near Plymouth Colony, we might not be here today having *this* feast of thanksgivin.'"

"Those Indians remind me of my Indian friends in No-Man's-Land and the Carolinas. William Bradford wrote a proclamation as Governor of the colony three years later that contained these words: 'Thanksgiving to ye Almighty God for all His blessings.' We need to do the same today, and I think it would be nice to have this celebration every year. Let's make it a tradition!"

"I gave the blessin' and sat down next to William. I noticed a light-skinned slave who was servin' lemonade. I also recognized her from church the week before. She would not look up, nor did she speak to anyone—except Platt. Her face had no life. She did her work, but it was as if someone had ripped out her joy.

After some small talk with William, I said, "I'd also like to speak to your female slave. I saw her at church last week."

With a questioning glance, William wrinkled up his sun-tanned forehead and looked at me. "Oh, you mean Dradey?"

"Yes, William. Platt intrigues me, but your Dradey . . . Well, she makes my heart hurt, and I want to know why her pain grieves the Spirit within me."

Conversation durin' our meal was most lighthearted. Miss Elvy sat close beside me and joined in on most topics that the other women dared not venture into. Samuel and Aimuewell sat right across the table and ate like field hands before they asked to be excused to go swim in Hurricane Creek. There were three older boys who volunteered to watch the children swim, so we had little concern. The food before us was delicious, and there were many choices, from the corn bread and biscuits to the mouth-waterin' ham with all the fixin's, and finally my favorite, dewberry pie.

The table talk was mostly about newly acquired livestock: our school, Spring Creek Academy; the death of President William Henry Harrison from pneumonia earlier that year; the new President, "His Accidency" John Tyler; family; and what the members at Spring Hill Baptist were going to do about the Campbellites. A couple times, the conversation drifted, mostly because of two men, toward how the slaves needed to be kept in line and disciplined. William quickly changed the discussion each time. I think he did it for the sake of our children and womenfolk sittin' there.

After we finished eatin', everyone got up and went back to minglin'. Miss Elvy and I stopped to talk with William's brother-in-law, Peter Tanner, who was speakin' to Edwin Epps and Jim Burns from over Bayou Boeuf way about the necessity of the whip and how the Bible condoned the use of *stripes*. For Miss Elvy's sake, I made the excuse of checking on our boys, but not before Mr. Epps reminded me that we had once met at Bennett's Store on Bayou Boeuf. Neither of us felt comfortable with the conversation.

As we left that conversation, we met Robert and Ruth Graham, who told us they had just moved from Mississippi to Forest Hill on Barber Creek 'bout a mile away. That creek had long been my refuge from the cares of life. After some talk 'bout the crops, children, and weather, I asked 'im,

"Are ya'll Baptist?"

"No," he responded, "we're Methodist."

"Seein's how there's no Methodist church nearby, ya might want to attend Spring Hill Baptist." We both laughed, and he agreed. There was somethin' 'bout 'im that I liked.

While Miss Elvy went off to see what Samuel and Aimuewell were doin', I saw William speakin' to Platt. I made my way over to 'em, and William saw me comin'. He stopped and said, "Pastor, I would like you to meet Platt, a mighty good worker and a fine musician."

"Platt, it is a pleasure to meet you." I found myself peerin' into the weathered face of a well-muscled man of maybe thirty years. His eyes were bright and didn't miss a thing. His long fingers easily held his fiddle and bow in one hand. For several seconds, we stood there just lookin' at each other.

"Pastor, it's nice to meet you too, sir."

William said, "I'm going to be right over here talkin' to some friends from Beulah Baptist over in Cheneyville."

"I just nodded. "That will be tolerable." I wasn't sure what he thought was goin' to happen.

After William moved away, I said to Platt, "You're a good fiddler and, well . . . I want to know more 'bout ya."

"Pastor, I am not sure what to say. I have almost been beaten to death in the slave pens for tellin' the truth, and my heart beats me up for tellin' lies about who I really am."

"Not your Master Ford?"

"No sir, no, Pastor, there has never been a more kind, noble, Christian man than Master Ford. He has never laid a hand on me or any of the others."

"What's your given name?"

"I'm not supposed to tell ya that."

"If anyone asks, tell 'em I insisted."

"My name is Solomon Northup."

"Do ya mind if I call you by your real name?" Solomon did not respond quickly. "Listen, if anyone has a problem with that, tell 'em to take it up with me."

I watched his hand clutch his fiddle more tightly, and the look in his eyes changed. There was an intensity that could not be ignored, and it seemed he wanted to say somethin'.

He finally spoke with a hushed but strong voice. "Pastor, I heard you speak last Sunday at church 'bout the advice your mama gave you when you had a decision to make. I have but one question for you."

"What's that, Solomon?"

He laid down his shiny fiddle and bow, untucked his shirt, pulled it up, and turned to show me his back. "What would your Jesus do about this?"

William must have seen this exchange by the surprised look on his face. He quickly came over and spoke to Solomon. "What are you doin'? Pull your shirt down, and show respect to Pastor Willis."

"William, he has done nothin' wrong."

"Platt, please go and continue playin' for our guests." William's voice was commanding.

"Yes, sir, I will do exactly that." He tucked his white cotton shirt into his trousers and got himself ready to play his tunes. Before he moved on, our eyes met again, and the unspoken words between us hung heavy."

Dan, his back carried deep, ugly stripes from the slave pens that reminded me of another's stripes—our Savior's.

I watched Solomon standin' up straight and tall, playin' his fiddle, and I heard all kinds of music, from hymns to the Virginia reel. He had a confidence that could only come from a good upbringin'. He was like no slave I'd ever met.

I didn't know what to say when he asked, "What would Jesus do?"

William said, "Pastor, you're missin' the pie-eatin' contest. Are you sure nothin's wrong?"

"No, William, all is favorable. By the way, would you mind if I come to Spring Hill to deliver the message next Sunday mornin'?"

"Of course not. We'd be honored. I know I can speak for the others."

"Good! I'm gonna walk down to Hurricane Creek for a spell. I need to talk with my mama!" William looked puzzled.

"Great-Grandpa, what 'bout Mr. Ford's slave, Dradey? Did you get a chance to talk to her? Did you find out why she was so sad?"

"There was no good time to talk to her that day in private. When I went to minister to her a couple days later, her story changed everything!"

16

Dan, the ride out to William's plantation was an agreeable one, and I arrived mid- mornin'.

We greeted each other on the porch before he invited me in for coffee. His wife, Martha, had made some coffee cake earlier, and the aroma still lingered as we surveyed his property from the second floor of the porch.

"Pastor, I didn't expect to see you quite so soon, but it is always good to have you visit."

"Remember last Saturday when I said I wanted to meet your slave, Dradey? I am here to minister to her. Her heart is very heavy. Can you find her for me?"

"I think she's down in a cabin. She's feelin' poorly today." William looked curious and confused.

"Do you mind showin' me which cabin?"

"Of course not, Pastor. Let's just walk down and see her." We walked through a small orchard of pear, peach, and orange trees and down a narrow path to a group of shotgun slave cabins.

When we reached the second cabin, he called out, "Dradey? Dradey, come on out here."

The door opened slowly, and she walked out, wipin' her hands on her dress. "Yes, sir?"

"Pastor Willis is here to talk with you. You heard 'im preach last week at church." William stood there and made no effort to leave.

"William, I mean no disrespect, but it's best I minister to her *alone*." I knew that she would not speak openly in his presence. He had little choice but to humor me, though I'm sure he wanted to stay and hear her words.

It took William a few minutes to make his way back to the house. I studied her tear-stained face. "Do you mind if we sit here and visit for a spell?" I asked. She eyed me with suspicion as she sat down in a rockin' chair. She shrugged and finally gave an approvin' nod.

I sat on the top step of the weather-rotted porch, and she immediately clutched her knees and put her head down, starin' at the sparse grass in the little yard.

"Mr. Ford told me your name is Dradey. Is that your given name? What's your Christian name?"

"No, sir. My name is Eliza."

"I'm goin' to call you Eliza, if you don't mind. Eliza! That's a special name to me. I have a granddaughter and a great-granddaughter named Eliza." She stared at me with uncertainty.

"Eliza, I'm not sure what happened to you, but I know someone who can heal your broken heart." She said nothin' but commenced rockin' back and forth, and not in a comfortable way. "Eliza, you can talk to me. I want to pray for you and help you if I can."

"Pastor, if that *someone* you speak of really had loved me, He would not have allowed my babies to be torn from my arms. I'm mad at God!"

"Eliza, I have felt that way before, but why do you feel like that?' Her broken heart seemed to split wide open, and she poured out her soul between her groans and sobs. 'My former owner in Maryland, Master Berry, was good to me and my children! He was very kind, and he took good care of us. I worked hard to please 'im and was rewarded with special gifts, nice clothes, and extra food for me and my children. He's the daddy to my two children, Randall and Emily. He loved 'em like a daddy should. He spoiled 'em too much with candy and toys.

"His daughter Jane was jealous of that. She acted like we were stealin' somethin' from her. She hated us with a passion and wanted us gone. While Master Berry was away from home, Miss Jane and her friend Jacob Brooks told me that my freedom papers were ready to sign. It was a dream come true that my two babies and me were goin' to be free at last. They told me to get in the wagon so we could get freedom papers for all three of us. I could hardly believe my ears. I packed up our clothes, and Randall, Emily, and me got into the back of the wagon.

"Seemed like we were goin' in the wrong direction, but I was so excited that I said nothin'. Wasn't far when the driver pulled the wagon over and got down. He walked to the back and grabbed our bag of clothes. He grinned and threw 'em into the nearby stream, shouting, 'Ya'll won't be needin' this where you're goin'!'

"I screamed and started to stand up, but the other man in the front threatened to hit me. He said, 'You're going for a little ride, and you're gonna keep quiet or I will do things to you that you won't like.' I realized we weren't goin' to be freed. I pulled my Randall and Emily close to me, cryin', 'Oh, Lord, help us!' The tobacco-chewin' man spat and grunted at me, 'You're gonna need all the prayers you can get, nigger!' "My children held onto me for dear life. I spoke lovin' words and sang some of their favorite songs to keep 'em calm. They cried, 'Mama, where are we goin'?' Randall cried, 'Mama, we ain't got no clothes to wear, and that mean man threw away our toys!' I felt hopeless as the daylight disappeared. The night brought me no comfort, except that my babies slept peacefully beside me.

"Preacher, we came to what looked like a big city and pulled up to an old buildin'. The two men started yellin', 'Get 'em up and get 'em down here.' A man walked up to the door and knocked loudly. When the door opened, we were shoved through, and a scary, dirty, old man told us to sit down. He was sweaty, with only a few teeth, and he scared Randall and Emily. Preacher, he grabbed my Randall and pulled 'im away from me. He cried, 'Mama, help me. Help!'

"The old slaver man pushed Randall through another door. Emily and I were taken to a cold, damp room. As I held my sweet girl that night, lookin' at her innocent little face, I prayed, 'God, don't let this happen to my children.' Both of us were kept in this dirty room for several days. We were given just enough stale bread and water to survive. I gave mine to Emily.

"A few days later, we were brought outside to clean up. On the way, I heard my Randall's voice. I started runnin' toward him, and he hugged me ever so tightly. The slavers were very rough and cracked the whip about too much talkin'. They wanted us to clean up, and we obeyed. That night, eight or nine of us includin' my children were put into another wagon, covered up, and taken to a river, to the biggest steamboat I had ever seen. My children and I walked up the stage plank, and we were then taken down to the belly of the boat. Most of the slaves were men. When they saw my children, the sad looks on their faces told the story, and my stomach turned. That night, we slept in a corner where Randall curled up on one side of me and Emily slept on the other. The churnin' of the boat put 'em to sleep.'

"That river ride lasted several days. I had met Solomon Northup in the slaver's yard a few days before. He gave my hungry babies what little food and water he had. The stench in the boat's belly made us all sick. When the steamer stopped, we were taken to another slave pen worse than the first, and the next mornin' we were ordered out into the yard to wash ourselves. They threatened us with a whip to make us move faster. We were given clean clothes to wear and oil to make our skin shine.

"I cuddled my dear babies and told 'em, 'Mama loves you.'

"Another of the slavers named Burch, dressed in a *fine* suit said, 'Now we go to market.'

"For a moment, Randall and Emily smiled as they remembered how Mr. Berry used to buy 'em candy at a market."

"Like I said, today is the day some of you will meet your new masters. Look good, step lively, and remember that I am watching every move you make. There will be a price to pay for disrespect or the like."

We were taken into a room where many fancy-dressed men were walkin' 'round. Some had their wives, but they just followed along behind. The men were touchin' us, lookin' in our mouths as they would a horse, and feelin' our arms and legs for strength. They separated us, with the men on one side and women on the other. I heard one plantation owner say he was from Natchez and that he had bought David and Caroline, who had come down the river with us. That's when I learned we were on the Mississippi River. Then he moved along the line and stopped and looked at Randall. He went to speak with the slave trader, Freeman. It became clear what was going to happen to my baby. I started cryin' out to that man to buy us as a family.

I promised 'im, "I'll work very hard and cause you no trouble. Just don't take my baby from me." Freeman came at me with his whip raised. I didn't quit. "Please, I beg you. Take us all. Don't take my boy from me. He's but ten years old. He needs his mama. He'll work harder if I am there."

My tears and words did not change their minds. I could do nothin' to save 'im. I ran to 'im and kissed his sweet face over and over again. "Be a good boy, Randall. Do as you're told." Freeman was yellin' at me while his other two men pulled Randall from my arms.

"I will, Mama! Don't cry, Mama! I'll be good." Those were the last words I heard 'im say.

Eliza stopped and looked at me with a grimace on her tear-stained face. "Preacher?"

"Yes, Ma'am?"

"You asked, 'What would Jesus do?' in your sermon last week. Where was *your* Jesus that day? Why didn't He do somethin'?"

Miss Eliza could not contain her grief. She wailed and sat there, wringin' her hands. My heart ached as I pictured what had happened to her. I had no answer for her question.

✤ ✤ ✤

Dan's eyes were huge as he listened to Eliza's story. "Great-Grandpa, did she ever see her son again? What happened to her daughter?"

"Dan, I'm not sure I ought to tell ya that part. I want to see what your father thinks."

17

August 18, 1841
WILLIAM PRINCE FORD'S WALLFIELD PLANTATION
ON HURRICANE CREEK
NEAR FOREST HILL, LOUISIANA

Father, please tell Great-Grandpa that I'm old enough. I'm already thirteen . . . and a half."

The elder Daniel spoke: "Grandpa, I think he is old enough, and I want to hear it, too."

"All right then, Dan, where was I? Just when Eliza's story seemed not to be able to get worse, it did."

✤　✤　✤

No one bought Emily and me that day, so we were sent back to the slave pen. During the night we all got real sick, and they took us to the hospital. The doctor said Emily and me had smallpox. I prayed that Randall didn't catch it, too. Solomon Northup was the most sick.

It took us a few weeks to gain our strength back, but when we did, we were sent back to the slave pen. Burch told us how mad he had been when we had not made a good enough showin' on that first day for the plantation owners. "You niggers are costin' me money! Now, do it right this time, or else." After he threatened to beat us, we were told to act better, but I had no strength to obey.

My heart ached for Randall, and I missed 'im so much. Emily clung to my hand as we made our way into the market house again.

A different group of people came, and the talk was louder. Freeman tapped me on the shoulders, tellin' the buyers, "Come, see her arms! She can pick lots of cotton for ya. And work your sugarcane fields, too."

A man entered the room and started lookin' around. He did not touch any of us but rather spoke calmly and asked questions. "Can you cook? Can you pick cotton?"

I told 'im, "I am a good mother. Please take both my daughter and me. I will be a good slave for you, and I'll never run away. Just take us both, mister."

He moved on into the next room. Freeman came roarin' at me. "What did you say to Mr. Ford?" "I told him I would be a good slave."

"You must have said somethin' to make 'im leave."

"No sir, I said nothin' wrong."

"See to it that ya don't."

Another plantation owner came in and started starin' at Emily. My soul cried out. I thought I would pass out, but I knew I had to be strong for Emily. That is when Master Ford returned and talked to Freeman. He pointed to Solomon and a couple more, and then he pointed to me.

I started speakin' quietly, but I could hear my voice gettin' louder and louder. I pleaded with 'im, "Please, sir, you *must* take me and my daughter together. We're family. They have already taken my son, and I cannot bear losin' my only other child. I beg you, for the love of God, take us both."

I dropped to my knees and pleaded for mercy. Little Emily began to cry. The other man stepped up and made Freeman an offer for Emily but was told, "She is not for sale. I am going to keep the girl, and someday, she will bring me a good income."

Master Ford said in a loud enough voice for all to hear, "Have you no compassion for this woman? What does it hurt you to sell the both of 'em to me?"

"Mr. Ford, this is business, and it would hurt my finances."

With that, Master Ford shook his head and pulled out his money and paid. I was not sure who he had bought until Freeman's men came to take me away. I thrashed about as Emily held me tightly. The men pinned my arms behind me so I was unable to even hug her. I bent over and kissed her face and told her, "Mama loves you very much."

Freeman's men pushed me, and they pulled my baby away from me. Emily was hollerin' for me, and I tried to get to her but Freeman was holdin' her in his grip. He had a most evil smile on his face. She was my precious angel.

Preacher, my heart breaks for my children, day and night. I talk to Randall and Emily every day, but they're not here to talk back. Solomon has told me that I should stop this, but no one can make me stop missin' 'em or lovin' 'em!

We were then taken to Master Ford's wagon and brought here. I have prayed to die ever since."

Anger rose up in her words that caused me to remain quiet. "So, Preacher, I heard your message last week. Your mama sounds like she was a wise woman. I have no decision to make, 'cause I'm dying inside, but I'm asking ya again, where was your Jesus, Preacher?"

I remained silent. Dan, I still had no answer for her.

She continued, "Why doesn't Jesus bring my children back? That Book in your hands says He won't put on us more than we can bear. I can't bear anymore."

She was weepin' too hard to continue. I turned and walked back to William's house and found him sittin' on the front porch, waitin' for me. I felt as if all the blood had been drained from me.

"Great-Grandpa, can ya tell me the rest of what happened?"

"Dan, it's gettin' late. Tomorrow, we'll sit outside in the sunshine, and I'll tell you what Mr. Ford said."

Young Dan was up waitin' for his great-grandfather when Joseph let 'em know he was ready to come out for breakfast. After some fresh chicory coffee, buckwheat pancakes, and bacon, Joseph felt renewed and prepared to continue. Lemuel and Dan carried him outside to the porch and covered 'im with his lap blanket.

"Great-Grandpa, I'm ready."

Lemuel and Daniel both spoke, "We are, too!"

"Not sure I'm ready, but here we go. . . . "

18

August 18, 1841

WILLIAM PRINCE FORD'S WALLFIELD PLANTATION

ON HURRICANE CREEK

NEAR FOREST HILL, LOUISIANA

I could hardly speak to William as we sat on his front porch. He seemed shocked.

"Pastor, you look like you've seen a ghost."

"Maybe I have, William. Maybe I have."

"Why don't you have a seat and rest for a while. How was your visit with Dradey?"

"It was . . . um, interestin'!"

"Were you able to help her any?"

"I don't think so."

"Really? Why not?"

"I'm not rightly sure why." I noticed that William was not lookin' at me as his eyes looked over his plantation. "William, can you tell me what happened a few months back, when you were in N'Orleans to buy your new slaves?"

He sighed. "Pastor, I arrived in N'Orleans the day before the slave market opened and stayed in an inn that night. It was a short business trip so I could get me some slaves to help with the lumber mill and a couple to take care of pickin' cotton and other crops around here. Martha had asked for someone to help in the house, too.

"The next mornin', I went over to Mr. Freeman's slave market. When I got there, Platt was playin' the fiddle and doin' a right fine job. I decided first to settle on a female house slave for my Martha. I saw Dradey there with her little girl. I went to Mr. Freeman and asked how much he wanted for the both of 'em.

"He shook his head and said, 'Mr. Ford, the young girl is not for sale. I'm gonna get $5,000 someday for her. Are you willin' to pay that today? If not, I might just keep 'er for myself for a while, then sell 'er when she's a tad bit older. Ain't she a pretty little thing? With that light skin, green eyes, and brown hair, she'll grow up nice for what I have planned. Mr. Ford, like it or not, the plaçage system is recognized in these here parts. It's the law in N'Orleans. Her bein' mixed race might just make some gentlemen a nice placées. I'm doin' it for 'er as well as just tryin' to make a meager livin'. It's the Christian thing to do, don't ya think? That way, she might even become a free person of color someday.'

"Pastor, I do not believe that his intentions were honorable. I went there to buy seven slaves, and altogether it wouldn't have cost me $5,000. I was spendin' $1,000 for Platt, and Freeman was willing to sell me Dradey for $700. I only had $3,500 with me. I didn't have any more money."

We sat quietly—neither of us was able to speak. William's head was low, as was his heart.

"William, where is Solomon? I want to speak with 'im."

"Solomon?"

"You know, Platt. His given name is Solomon."

He looked surprised and took a minute to answer. "He's at my lumber mill but comin' home very soon."

"I'll sit here and wait for 'im, if you don't mind."

"That will be fine. Do you want me to wait with you?"

I patted his knee. "Of course William, please stay. It's your home."

We sat there in silence and rocked quietly until Solomon led a small group of men back from the lumber mill. He seemed lost in his thoughts as William called his name.

"Platt, please come here. Pastor Willis would like a few words with ya."

95

He stopped for a few seconds, then left the others and came toward the house. I stood and went down the two steps and stood in front of 'im.

Solomon said, "Pastor?"

I glanced back at William and then at Solomon and said, "How about you walk with me? I'd like to ask you a few questions."

He looked toward his master for approval, and William nodded. We walked down to Hurricane Creek. "Solomon, I talked to Eliza today."

Solomon's eyes flashed at me. "Did she tell you everythin'?"

I told Solomon all that she had said and asked 'im if there was anything he could add.

"That's most of it, Pastor, but there was a couple more things. She was beside herself with grief and fear for her little girl. Rightly so! Master Ford went to talk with Freeman and offered to buy 'em both, but Freeman was determined to make her a quadroon. The other slaves told me that she would be raised as a white woman for evil men's pleasures.

"Dradey has cried every day and talks to her babies like they were right beside her. Don't think she's right in her mind anymore. She don't eat and sits and rocks back and forth. She's no good for Mistress Martha in the house. Pastor, I've never seen anyone so sad."

Solomon put his head down and stared at the ground, shakin' his head. We walked back in silence to the house, where William dismissed Solomon for the day. I thanked William for his hospitality and told 'im I was lookin' forward to seein' 'im on Sunday mornin'. Dan, I was most grateful to get on Ole Sally and head for home. It had been a very long, hard day.

Lemuel and Daniel hung on every word that Joseph spoke, and as morning wore on, no one seemed to care about the time. Young Dan's puzzled face showed concern as Joseph took off his lap blanket and asked for help to make it back inside to rest a spell.

"But, Great-Grandpa, did ya ever find out what Jesus would do?"

"Dan, I'm gettin' to that."

19

Dan, to finish answering your questions, I saddled Ole Sally Saturday mornin' and spoke to her as I was gettin' ready. 'This is the day which the Lord hath made. We will rejoice and be glad in it.' Her look was strange enough to make me laugh. I had gotten up at the first crow of my new Dominicker rooster. Only five months old, he already sounded as loud as Gabriel blowin' his horn. I had to head over to speak at Spring Creek Academy.

"William Prince Ford was the president of the school's board of trustees. He had told me that the principal, Joseph Eastburn, had requested I come and speak to the children. I told William I'd come if I could tell 'em stories from the Bible. I understood that when the legislature chartered the school in 1837, they insisted no one could be refused admission for their religious tenets. I wanted to be sure my stories would be all right with 'em. William said that would not be a problem."

Dan asked, "Great-Grandpa, did you forget I go there now? I heard that the plantation owners send their children there to keep 'em from getting diseases and fevers."

"That may be true. The academy is far enough away from the riverboats that are said to have spread cholera, malaria, and yellow fever. They wanted the school situated at some healthy point on Spring Creek, but still close enough to the Texas Road so they could get to the school from their plantations on Bayou Boeuf and as far away as Orleans Parish.

"The planters have come here for years from their bottomland as a refuge from the summer heat and the diseases that have plagued 'em there. William was smart enough just to move here, even though his wife, Martha, owns 200 acres on Bayou Boeuf across from her brother, Peter Tanner.

"As we made our way on the short ride to the school, Ole Sally and me took a slight detour so I could water her with the ice-cold waters of Barber Creek. The creek was so clear I could have dropped my open Bible in it and read it from the bottom. It was here that I always went to clear my mind.

"The sounds of the forest 'round me took me far away from the cares of life. All week, I had carried a heavy burden. As I stood there and listened, I was reminded of the words the Lord spoke to the old prophet Isaiah: 'And thine ears shall hear a word behind thee, saying, this is the way, walk ye in it. . . . '

"I fell to my knees on the sandy banks of Barber Creek. 'Lord Jesus, how would You have me answer Solomon and Eliza? What would You have me do? Let the things that break Your heart break mine.' I knelt there but for a moment, then got up and brushed the sand off my knees and said, 'Yes, Lord, break my heart, but You don't have to answer the question of slavery again. You have taught me in the way I was to walk and answered that question for me and my mother by Your Word and Your Spirit on the banks of another river many years ago—the Cape Fear. Forgive me, Lord, for forgettin' from whence I came. You have said 'I'm no longer a slave, for a slave does not know what his master is doing. You have said that I am now a friend and a joint heir with You. I am no longer a slave, not once, not twice—not ever again. Nor should any man be!'

"My mind was as clear as Barber Creek now, and my heart was once again at peace. I journeyed on to the school. After I told 'em Bible stories, Mr. Eastburn invited me to spend the night there because he knew I was speakin' at Spring Hill Baptist the next mornin'. I thanked 'im and told 'im that William Prince Ford had already invited me to stay at his home."

"Great-Grandpa, what Bible story did ya tell 'em?"

"One of my favorites about David and Goliath. I told 'em that someday they would have giants in their lives, too. Might be a person, or a disease like yellow fever. When I got all done, one little boy named Josh stood up and said, 'Pastor, that's really good!' I've never forgotten his response."

After leavin' the school, I whispered in one of Ole Sally's big ears, "I think we should sleep on the ground in the piney woods tonight, like we used to. What do you think?" She gave me another one of her mulish looks. "Yup. Just as I thought. You want to have some time in the Lord's creation rather than that barn, don't ya, ole girl?"

Spendin' the night at the academy or at Mr. Ford's place was not where I wanted to be. I had a strong desire to sleep under the tall longleaf pines. It had been a very long time since I'd slept under the stars, and this was an evenin' for doin' exactly that.

The principal's wife had given me some food to take with me. We were only a stone's throw from Hurricane Creek.

It was but a short time before Ole Sally and I found a perfect spot on the banks of Hurricane Creek, a short ride from the church. Since my early days in the Louisiana Territory, I have found solace with the peaceful sounds of the piney woods. The lowest branches of those majestic longleaf pines were at least fifty feet off the ground, and I could see a long ways off 'cause there was no underbrush. The trees' canopy kept it from growin', for there was little light even at high noon. I could have run Ole Sally at a full lope through those pines without fear of hittin' anything. But, those days had long since passed for the both of us. The plentiful pine straw had all the makin's for a soft bed, and the rich aroma brought back wonderful memories of my early days in this land that I've called home for nearly a half-century now.

For the longest time, I did not make a fire. I just sat there on the banks of the creek, listenin' and watchin'. A large whitetail buck wandered by not far from us, headed down toward the creek for some cold water. He looked proud, and my presence did not spook him. It reminded me of David's words in the Psalms, when he spoke of a deer pantin' for water like David's soul panted for the Lord. Oh, how I understood that longin', especially on that day.

I watched the gray squirrels chasin' each other round the trees and buryin' pine knots and heard the howl of a lone coyote. There was also the sound of a panther screamin', like the sound of a woman screamin' in the distance, and an old black bear growlin' 'n makin' noise, but there was no fear that day, nor any darkness in my heart throughout the soon-to-be night.

I led Ole Sally down to the creek and stood there on the bank, watchin' the brim snappin' at the skimmers and listenin' to the crickets and bull-frogs. A mama raccoon and her three babies came to the creek's edge on the other side and dipped their little paws into the cold water. I was most thankful to God for all His blessin's. I thanked Him for the splendor of Louisiana and the peace and beauty it had given me for many years now. "You are the Lord of Creation. You alone are!"

"After makin' a small fire with pine cones for kindlin' to warm my supper, I leaned back 'gainst a pine tree and did some thinkin' 'bout my early days here. There were no inns and few people. I first came to the Louisiana Territory back in 1798 and slept under the stars, where I got to know most of the animal sounds and bird calls.

I was so near Hurricane Creek that I could hear the clear water gurglin' and slippin over the gravel. The moon slowly made its way across the sky, and I could have read the Good Book without a candle as it crossed the narrow clearin' in the creek's path.

As the moon passed on, the stars came out and lit up the sky. I agreed with the shepherd boy who became a king: "The heavens declare the glory of God, and the firmament sheweth his handiwork."

I gathered up lots of pine straw and pulled my blanket out of my saddlebag. All I could say was, "Lord, You are sweeter than the honey-comb that black bear was just eatin'!" I felt the peace that passeth all understandin' come over me, and I slept like a newborn baby.

The next mornin', I woke to the sound of a couple of loud green-head mallards and the most unusual sound of blue herons tellin' of the crawfish they'd just found. I felt fully rested as I got up and went down to the creek to wash up. I knew it was early, 'cause the sun hadn't climbed up far in the eastern sky. There were the faintest hints of red and orange mixed in the clouds, meanin' a storm was brewin', but hopefully not too soon.

I ate a couple of biscuits with mayhaw jelly and warmed up the coffee from the night before. Ya know, Dan, there is somethin' special 'bout a cup of Louisiana coffee in these here piney woods. It was a great way to start the mornin', and the peace of the forest was only surpassed by the peace in my heart. I collected my things and rode Ole Sally over to Spring Hill Baptist Church. When I got there, I could see that people were already beginnin' to arrive. It looked like the attendance was goin' to be good.

20

SPRING HILL BAPTIST CHURCH ON HURRICANE CREEK
NEAR FOREST HILL, LOUISIANA

I watched William Prince Ford ride up and tie his saddle horse to one of the hitchin' rails next to Ole Sally. He smiled and said, "Mornin', Pastor. We missed you last night. Looks like another great day at Spring Hill. You look rested this mornin'."

"Yes, William, sorry we did not make it to your place yesterday, but thank you for the invitation. We decided to sleep under the stars. It was refreshin'!" We started walkin' toward the church. "William, ya know the other day, when we were talkin' about Eliza, or, as you know her, Dradey?"

"Yes, sir."

"I thought of another question yesterday down on Barber Creek."

"What was that, Pastor?"

"Why did you buy Eliza after he refused to sell you Emily?"

He looked puzzled. "I don't know, Pastor. I never thought of that."

We kept walkin', but he slowed down and asked, "Did I do something wrong, Pastor? What would you have done differently?"

Dan, this is when I told 'im how the mule ate the cabbage.

I pointed to Ole Sally. "See that old mule goin' grey like me? I'd have climbed on her back, and we would've caught a fast steamboat at Alex first to N'Orleans and then to Natchez. I would have then found her children. Come Hades or high water, I would have raised the money for 'em and given them back to their mama. In fact, I would have never bought Eliza without her daughter—and as of yesterday, I would not have bought either of 'em in the first place."

William was about half a step behind me as we walked up to the front door, and I could tell he wanted to say more.

Inside the people greeted us warmly. "Nice to see you, Mr. Ford."

Peter Tanner shook my hand. "Can't wait to hear your sermon, Pastor."

Another added, "Isn't this a nice day!" I smiled at the folks, but William didn't respond to their interruptions, and his red face carried an expression that was hard to describe.

As I was makin' my way down the aisle and greetin' people, he came up behind me and said, "Pastor, you're beginnin' to sound like one of those abolitionists from the Northern churches. You're not 'gainst slavery, are you?"

I turned and replied over my shoulder, "You might be onto somethin' there, William."

By then, I was at the front and ready to sing some hymns. I thought, *If ever I needed to be in the Spirit, it's right now.* My eyes looked 'round the sanctuary for Solomon and Eliza and I was happy to see that they were there. He was sittin' with the men slaves, and she was seated with the women slaves at the back of the church, for there was no balcony.

After the singin', I got up and read the scripture about the Golden Rule. "Which of you children can recite the Golden Rule?" I asked.

A young boy sittin' next to Peter Tanner stood to his feet and said, "Treat others the way you want to be treated."

"That's very good. It says, 'Therefore all things whatsoever ye would that men should do to you, do ye even so to them: for this is the law and the prophets.' I just spoke yesterday at your school...." All the children clapped. "Can you tell me what that verse means?"

Another young boy raised his hand and stood. "Pastor, it means that however I treat others is goin' to come back on me, like if I'm mean to someone during recess, they're gonna be mean back to me." Everyone nodded in agreement.

"Well said, young man. That's one way to look at it." The boy sat down. "Now, let me ask you adults, how many of *you* believe in the Golden Rule?" All hands went up, and everyone was lookin' 'round.

"Good. My next question is, 'Who's your brother?'"

Peter Tanner stood and said, "Bible says that everyone is our brother."

"You have answered correctly, for Jesus' own half-brother, James, wrote in the Word of God that we are to treat everyone the same. My father told me many times that the test of a man's character is how he treats those who can do nothin' for 'im. Those who know me often hear me tell stories about my mama, who was a Cherokee slave. When I was facin' a big decision, she would always give me the same advice: 'Joseph, ask yourself the question, "What would Jesus do?"'

"I had to ask the Lord that question yesterday on Barber Creek. I fell to my knees and I asked Him, 'What would You have me do?' I then said, 'Lord, You don't have to answer that, because You gave me that answer already when I was a Cherokee slave many years ago, in my own family on my own property.' I grew up on the Cape Fear River in Bladen County, North Carolina. My father would often tell me, 'Joseph, see 'em boats? A risin' tide should lift all boats.' That's how he described the Golden Rule.

"The Lord then spoke to my heart yesterday, saying, 'My question to you, Joseph, is what are *you* going to do?' I'm now goin' to call a few men up to the front. Peter and William, would you mind comin' forward." Peter came forward quickly, but William was slow to cooperate.

"Gentlemen, would you mind showin' us your backs? Nothing immodest, please, but just lift your shirts a little.' The two men stood there stunned and did *not* do it. I then pulled out a whip from my bag. "Who would like to volunteer to lay one hundred stripes on the backs of these men?" The people gasped, and I saw a few women put their hands over their mouths.

"Do I have a slave who wants to whip these men for disobeying my request?"

No one moved. Not one person came forward to take the whip from my hand. I stood there, lookin' at the faces of these men and women I had known for a long time. Gentlemen, you may sit down now.

"I came here in 1798, and I have watched this sin called *slavery* grow, and I have done nothin' to stop it. I have not spoken out against the horrible treatment of my brothers and sisters. I have allowed God's Word to be used against 'em. I have heard the tragic stories of families being torn apart and of lost children, and I have sinned by my silence. I was once a slave, but never again, and neither should any other man be!"

With that, Peter Tanner stormed down the aisle and pulled his wife out of the pew. In his anger, he grunted, "This preacher is senile and has lost his mind. I am not staying for any more of this nonsense." Several more got up and walked out after 'im. But, to my surprise, most did not. I continued standing there, holdin' my whip. The thunder that boomed outside was not as loud as inside. The storm clouds had opened, and the rain pelted me in more ways than one as I left the church. I did see Solomon noddin' ever so slightly, and when I saw Eliza, her eyes were dry, and she seemed to be praisin' the Lord.

The news of my message spread throughout Rapides Parish like a wildfire. I was one of the most talked about men in Central Louisiana, but I was at peace.

"Great-Grandpa, didn't that scare you?"

"Not hardly. The Lord has brought me through many trials and tribulations. Wasn't sure how He'd do it this time, but I had faith He would again."

"So, what happened, Great-Grandpa?"

Joseph laughed and said, "That's a fine story for tomorrow. Let's go inside so I can rest a spell. I'm getting' hungry, too."

"Ah, Great-Grandpa, I just want to know if they hurt you."

"Pray for patience, son."
"I have, and I asked for it right now, too!"

21

Now, Dan, to get to your question from last night, several weeks passed since I'd spoken at Spring Hill Baptist, and the dust had not settled easily. 'Bout mid-mornin', there was a knock on my door, and there stood William, along with clergy from the Methodist, Presbyterian, Baptist, and the Disciples of Christ churches.

I invited 'em in and asked Miss Elvy to make some coffee. I told 'em, "I have fresh-baked root chicory and was lookin' for some special occasion. Seems the longer I'm here, the more I've grown to like the bitter taste. Have a seat, gentlemen."

William started the conversation. "Pastor, don't ya wonder why all these men are here with me?"

"Not really, William, I figured the chances were pretty slim they all would want to become Baptist at once. My guess is it's 'bout what I said about slavery."

"I never knew your feelin's were that strong against slavery, Pastor. I've felt that slavery might be wrong for a long time."

All the men around the table nodded and offered hearty declarations of, "Amen," and "That's right!"

I said, "Gentlemen, I'm goin' to get to the heart of the matter. If this is how we really feel, then why have we sat by and watched this happen? I'd like to hear from each of you."

Each clergyman gave a different answer, but all of the answers reminded me of a Cajun boiling down hog head cheese. In this case, what it all boiled down to was money and tradition. Even though none of 'em were paid in a direct way by the plantation owners, their wages came from a path of control by 'em, either by cotton gin receipts or donations to their church or denomination.

The Presbyterian spoke: "We are a divided church over this issue, the North from the South. Since about 1830, everything has changed. They no longer pay us in cash but started payin' us in cotton gin receipts to remind us from whence our substance came. The only stores that will take the receipts are controlled by 'em, too. Since then, we have been well advised to support the plantations and not say a questionable word 'gainst the owners."

I added, "I predict we Baptists in the South will break away from our Northern Baptist brothers one day soon over this issue, too. Our Northern-based Home Mission Society has had grave issues with slave owners becomin' missionaries since its formation in 1832. Many of my fellow Baptists have wanted a separate Southern mission body since the very beginnin' in '32."

William sat forward on the edge of his chair. "Pastor, I heard what ya said about going to N'Orleans and Natchez. Everyone thinks I've got a lot of money, but I signed a bank note for my brother, and he can't pay it. I'm 'bout bankrupt.

"I've been thinkin' 'bout sellin' my slaves for a couple of reasons. One is financial, and the other is moral. Pastor, if you really want to find Dradey's children, I'll help you raise the money to reunite 'em. I must tell you, though, after you spoke a couple weeks ago, at Martha's request, I sold Dradey to another plantation. I'll probably have to sell my other slaves, including Platt, to pay my debts."

I could say nothin' as I looked at 'im in disbelief.

"Dradey was just too sick with grief to be of use to Martha."

I sighed and put my head down. The room remained silent until I spoke to the group. "Friends, when I was a young preacher, and even before I was ordained, I was influenced by the Great Awakenin' preacher George Whitefield. He could do no wrong in my eyes. I read the letters that he sent to Benjamin Franklin after Franklin printed 'em, and I was greatly influenced by his thinkin'. Gentlemen, excuse me for a moment. Let me find that letter. I have a copy of it in my box."

I then went to the mantle above the fireplace and pulled down my tin box. I unfolded the brittle, yellowed paper.

"Let me just relay what Reverend Whitefield wrote in 1740 to his friend, Mr. Franklin, about the plantation owners' treatment of their slaves. 'God has a quarrel with you for your abuse of and cruelty to the poor Negroes.'" I looked up and added, Mr. Franklin said of Whitefield, 'He excoriated the slave masters for mercilessly beating their laborers, and for failing to provide basic food and clothing for them. He also suggested that white Southerners were keeping the gospel of Christianity from the slaves for fear that salvation would make them restless for freedom.'

"Ya see, Whitefield thought they should be evangelized. That's why they took their slaves to church, and that's why the plantation owners do today. Whitefield believed that Negroes were the spiritual equals of whites, and that masters should not abuse their slaves. Gentlemen, I have always believed that, too.

"With all that said by Whitefield, he still believed it was all right to own slaves. In fact, he later owned a plantation with slaves. That's how many in the churches got the notion it was all right. I say to you all today, as Paul the Apostle said, 'Let God be true, but every man a liar.'"

The Presbyterian said, "Pastor, I read those articles, too. I thought it was all right, so I bought slaves. I treated 'em right, was kind, and took 'em to church. Like Whitefield, I thought it was acceptable in God's eyes."

One of the Baptists said, "Whitefield wasn't alone. Thomas Jefferson, the writer of our own Declaration of Independence, owned slaves. And, he's not alone either, eight out of our ten Presidents have own slaves."

I asked them again, "Gentlemen, how did we get to this point? Louisiana has become rich off the backs of slave labor, and it's wrong that I have not spoken out against it. I have sinned by omission. Not sure my words would have made a difference, but I know my silence has! Gentlemen, these are basically the same words I spoke a few weeks ago at Spring Hill, that have caused all this upheaval. I might add I knew it was wrong in my heart of hearts. How could I have become so numb to it when I had been a Cherokee slave as a boy? We must never follow the crowd and lose the fact that we are called to be salt and light. Salt can heal, but it can sting, too. Our words must sting the conscience of Louisiana and heal the victims of slavery. Light always drives darkness away. Let us purpose to be the light in this darkness. If we don't, and Louisiana does not repent of this injustice, we can rest assured that God's favor will be lifted, and His rod of judgment may well fall upon our land."

I looked deep into the eyes of the men that sat 'round the table and said, 'I believe we have gotten caught up in the religion of influence. I've watched worldliness and ambition break the spirit of our brothers and sisters whose skin is a different color. As a boy, I saw firsthand the arrogance of prejudice in my own family back in North Carolina because of my dark skin. Today, I see the same ungodly arrogance in some of our Louisiana neighbors and even a few of our own church members. I've seen it help destroy our nation's two great spiritual awakenings.

"Because we did not come together and voice our beliefs as the Body of Christ, the plantation owners have grown very rich, bought more slaves, and found bigger and better ways to get their cotton and sugar up North.

"It would appear that not only are our brothers and sisters slaves, but by tradition we are slaves as well. I do not say this to bring shame upon us. I speak the truth and do not know how to right this wrong. But, there is a wind startin' to blow—the wind of war. Mark my words, our children and our children's children will have to pay for our sins of silence."

No one spoke. Several of the men had tears in their eyes and others sat stoically tryin' to put my words into perspective.

The youngest pastor from the Disciples of Christ said, "Pastor, I agree with you totally, but I have a family to feed. I cannot speak my mind freely and still put food on my table. I love my wife, and I have eight children to think about. Our founder, Alexander Campbell, has written against the terrible treatment of slaves in his *Millennial Harbinger*, but there has been much opposition to its circulation in Louisiana, and he lives in Virginia, not here."

The Methodist added, "We all agree. It's a shame that there are so many denominations today. Even though there are some things that divide us, there're also many things that unite us."

I stood and spoke. "Ya know, Jesus healed the blind in different ways. He put spittle once on a blind man's eyes, and he could see. Another time he healed a blind man by usin' mud to anoint his eyes. And, Jesus even once just touched a blind man's eyes to give 'im his sight. In the religious age we live in today, out of that would have come three denominations: the spitites, the mudtites, and the touchites." Everyone laughed. "But seriously, gentlemen, we are surrounded by religion and spiritual blindness. The question is, 'What would Jesus do?'"

They all agreed.

"I believe slavery is a sin, and for the rest of my days, I'm goin' to speak out against it to any and all that will listen."

William's face showed grave concern. "Pastor, have you thought about what men like Epps and Burns might do to you?"

"William, fear and faith do not mix well. They're like oil and water. The most often-mentioned words in the Bible are 'Fear not'—over 350 times, I've been told. Even if harm did come to me, that would only hasten my graduation day to glory. If God is for you, who can be against you?'

I looked around at their faces and saw mixed expressions. I offered them more coffee and some jellyroll cake that Miss Elvy had baked early that morning. We talked about our families, the weather, and our churches—but not about slavery again that day.

❖　❖　❖

"Great-Grandpa, did Mr. Epps and Mr. Burns get mad at you?"

Joseph smiled. "You might say they were a little bothered by my words."

"What did you do?"

"I kept right on preachin' Jesus! In fact, it wasn't but two weeks later that I delivered a similar message at Amiable Baptist and got the same response. I couldn't stop doin' what God had called me to do."

"Great-Grandpa, how do you know if you're called to preach?"

"Son, if you can keep from it, then don't."

"Great-Grandpa, you believe every word in the Bible, don't you?"

"Son, every jot and tittle. Every single word from Genesis to the maps in the back . . . well, maybe not the maps.

"Now, there was a rumblin' among some of the plantation owners and they let me know that I was causin' trouble for 'em. They were fearin' there'd be another slave revolt. They never came in person—well, that is except one time, but sent messengers sayin', 'Pastor, if you continue, we will be forced to take actions against ya.'"

Dan's eyes were huge, and his expression was worried. "Grandpa, weren't ya 'fraid of 'em? What they'd do to ya?"

"Not hardly! Not even when William came to express his concerns."

"What'd he say to ya?"

"He told me he'd heard some talk out of Bayou Boeuf from Epps and Burnses that they'd already given me a warnin' to stop preachin' about this slavery thing. He said, 'They're gonna take action if you don't stop.' William studied my face and said, 'Pastor, you are my dearest friend and mentor. You've always treated me as a son. What are you goin' to do? I don't want any harm to come to you.'

"I answered, 'Tell 'em I'm preachin' at Calvary Baptist in Bayou Chicot this Sunday, right near 'em. Invite 'em to come, and tell 'em to bring a covered dish, for we'll be havin' supper on the grounds after church.'

"William shook his head and smiled. 'Pastor, I admire your courage.

I'm sure you realize that you will not be safe there.'"

"Great-Grandpa, what were they gonna do to ya?"

"Dan, it didn't matter what *they* had planned. It reminded me of one of my favorite stories in the Bible 'bout a man named Jehoshaphat. He was facing three mighty enemies. He couldn't have whipped even one of 'em. He called his people to fast and pray. Jehoshaphat prayed somethin' like this: 'Lord, I don't have the foggiest idea what to do, but my eyes are on You.'

"The Lord spoke words like this to Jehoshaphat: 'You don't need to fight in this battle, for the battle is no longer yours, but Mine.' Son, how many battles has the Lord lost?"

"None!"

"Neither would He this time!"

"But, Great-Grandpa, did ya do *anything*?"

Joseph smiled at Dan and calmly said, "I went down to Spring Creek, cut me a nice cane pole, and caught me a mess of brim for supper."

22

October 24, 1841
JOSEPH WILLIS' HOME ON SPRING CREEK
BABB'S BRIDGE, LOUISIANA

William rode up to Joseph's home early Sunday evening saying, "Pastor, may I have a moment with you? I know I'm interruptin' your day of rest, but this is real important."

"Come on in, William. Want some coffee, or perhaps a glass of buttermilk? Wish you had been here this mornin', 'cause Miss Elvy made her famous grits for breakfast. I sometimes feel I'm diggin' my grave with my fork with her fine cookin.'"

"Coffee only, Pastor, 'cause I been up a long time." He looked to see if Miss Elvy was in hearing range and leaned in close to speak. "Pastor, seems there's trouble headed your way. Peter Tanner rode all the way from Bayou Boeuf to my home yesterday. He personally wanted me to know what happened Friday when he went to Bennett's General Store. He had walked over to buy some cotton sacks when Epps and Burns came ridin' up. They didn't see Peter walkin' over the bridge on Bayou Boeuf from his home, but he heard enough of their conversation to know they got some evil plans for you."

Joseph looked a little shocked. "That right? I thought Peter was mad at me."

"Well, he is, sorta . . . 'bout the slavery issue, but he doesn't want any harm to come to you. He thinks of you as a 'pioneer,' and you have done a lot for everyone 'round here. That's why he came to tell Martha and me about what they're plannin.' Burns and Epps have concocted a plan to ambush ya. They're bringin' along a couple of riffraff they hired out of N'Orleans."

"William, when is all this comin' down?"

"When you leave for Amiable Baptist next Sunday, they are gonna ambush you on your way to church. They want to shut you up—for good."

Joseph got really quiet. "But, William . . . Miss Elvy, Samuel, and Aimuewell will be with me."

"That's right, Pastor. They are gonna ambush ya 'bout a quarter mile from here, and they don't care who else gets hurt."

Joseph took a deep breath as he motioned for Miss Elvy to join them at the table.

"Miss Elvy, seems there is goin' to be some unwanted visitors 'round here. You need to hear this.

"William, there have been two other times that the Lord has sent messengers to warn me of danger. Once was down in Vermilionville, when a friend, Jacques Cormier, warned me to flee because the religious folk there didn't like what I was preachin' and were gonna kill me to shut me up. Another was at an inn in No-Man's-Land when Malachi Perkins warned me to flee in the middle of the night 'cause two men were gonna ambush me for what little money I had. William, you are the third messenger to warn me of danger. You risked your life and reputation to come here today, and I want to thank you." Then Joseph was silent, letting all this sink in. 'I know it's time to leave and take Elvy and the boys across the Calcasieu to Tenmile Creek. William, we're gonna take the important things . . . but I'm leavin' one thing behind."

"Pastor, what's that?"

Joseph got up, walked to the mantle, and took down a large tin box and brought it over to the table, slowly opening it. "I started writin' down my journey in life many years ago, back in Bladen County, North Carolina, in this here journal. I want you to have it for future generations."

"But, Pastor, you have children who. . . . "

Joseph looked at him like a father correcting his son. "William, I have already spoken to my sons and daughters, and they're all in agreement that you should hold this diary. It's a journal of the history of the events in my life. You are an educated man, church clerk. You love history and you love the Lord. You are like a son to me." Joseph held the record in his hand as his fingers rubbed the familiar worn-leather cover.

William did not move quickly. "Pastor, I don't know what to say. I have learned much from you—you're my mentor. To think . . . your *entire life* is in this journal?"

"Hopefully, not yet. There's still work to be done, but I'm eighty-three, and I have no promise of tomorrow, at least not here. Take good care of it."

"I will, sir, I will!" Tears welled up in William's eyes, and he had to look away. "Now, Pastor, about next Sunday. . . . "

"I know!" Joseph sighed a breath of relief as he turned to Miss Elvy. "We need to start packin' soon."

William stood and walked to the door. Once outside, Joseph spoke. "William, I want to thank you again for comin' here today and warnin' me." William reached to give me the right hand of Christian fellowship, but Joseph pulled him in to give him a big bear hug. "And please, tell Peter I'm grateful for his help, too! I know this could put him in harm's way."

"Pastor, I will. Take good care of yourself and your family."

Joseph watched him ride off down the red-dirt road and 'round the bend.

Five days later, the Willises loaded up the wagon and took the ferry across the Calcasieu River. They went straight to Johnson Sweat's home on Tenmile Creek. When Joseph explained what had happened, Johnson said, "I just finished buildin' this new home, but my old house, the one where you came a-courtin' Miss Elvy, is empty. Why don't ya'll stay there?"

That next Saturday night, Epps, Burns, and the two scoundrels they'd hired from N'Orleans built their camp on Barber Creek, not far from my home. They were up and ready on Sunday mornin', but hours went by, and the Willises' wagon never rolled down the red-dirt road to church. After several uneventful hours, they decided to sneak up to Joseph's house and look 'round. It looked abandoned, but wagon tracks led toward the Calcasieu.

Dan, what happened next was the hand of the Lord. Two young boys from your school, Spring Creek Academy, were playin' hooky and swimmin' in Barber Creek when they thought saw some Indians. They heard all kinds of commotion just up around the bend of the creek and crawled up on a sandbar and laid on their bellies to see what the commotion was 'bout. What they saw was Epps and Burns and two other men changin' out of Choctaw disguises and puttin' their regular clothes back on. The men were angry and arguin'. They were yellin' and makin' bets about who had warned me about their plan. Thankfully, no one mentioned William or Peter.

The boys watched quietly, and one whispered, "That's Mr. Epps! My daddy told me 'bout him. He was at the feast of thanksgiving at Mr. Ford's plantation." Now, these boys were in a bit of a pickle, because they knew they'd be in trouble for playin' hooky if they told anyone what they had heard and seen. They also knew these men were up to no good. They did the right thing, though, and went and told their daddies.

The man who ran the ferry gave me some more of the story. He told me that after the men got back in their regular clothes, they rode back to follow the wagon tracks and discovered that they led to the ferry at the Calcasieu. The younger man from N'Orleans sat in his saddle and shook his head, sayin', "I ain't crossin' this here river. You're not paying me enough to go into No-Man's-Land." Epps and Burns just glared at 'em. Burns barked at the other man, 'You feel that way, too?"

"Yup! There are pirates, killers, and all kinds of bad ones over there."

"And you're not like any of 'em, right?" Burns had no time for their cowardly comments.

"Epps, let's give 'em part of the money and be done with 'em."

"Wait, we want what you promised to pay us—*all of it*," said the thinner man.

"But, you didn't do anythin'."

"It's not *our* fault that the preacher didn't show up."

Epps responded, "You better be glad to be gettin' away with your lives!" With that, Epps pulled his gun out and took aim. The two quickly found out that Burns and Epps were as bad as any bandits in No-Man's-Land.

It took Epps and Burns a couple days to ride back to Bayou Boeuf, but by then the news had already spread all the way to the Red River. Bless their hearts, after things began to heat up during the next several weeks, Epps and Burns denied takin' part in any plan to do me harm.

Everybody was talkin' 'bout what happened and how they'd been seen. They told everyone who was in earshot, "We ain't killers! We're Southern gentlemen and planters. We're good Christians, just like the preacher." They were smart enough to steer clear of the Spring Creek area, though.

All was real quiet in Tenmile Creek for about two weeks, until William came ridin' up again, but to our new home this time.

"William, it's good to see you again so soon!"

"You too, Pastor!" He slid off his saddle horse quickly as a man on a mission and tied his mare to a cedar tree. 'Remember what we talked about a couple of weeks ago, at your ole home place at Babb's Bridge? Do you mind if we talk again?"

I said, "I heard they came dressed as Choctaws. Heard, too, they were spotted changin' clothes on Barber Creek by some young'uns from the academy. They should've known it would take more than a fake Indian to sneak up on a Cherokee."

William eyed the stranger standing beside the pastor. "I don't mean to interrupt you and your guest. We can talk later."

The short, bearded man of about forty years spoke to William before Joseph could introduce them: "I hear tell that you're the third messenger."

William looked confused. "Pardon me?"

He continued, "I'm the second messenger, Malachi Perkins."

He put his whittlin' knife down, stepped toward William, and shook his hand. "Brother Ford, everybody knows 'bout what those scoundrels tried to do, and their dastardly conduct has spread from the Red to the Sabine Rivers. But now that the cat is out of the bag, they don't dare come around these here parts."

William spoke directly to Joseph. "That's true, but nobody knows what I'm fixin' to tell ya now. Pastor, these men are comin' for you again! Don't know how, but they're comin'!"

Malachi asked William, "How do you know this?"

"I don't know Epps or Burns very well, but Ezra Bennett sure does. They go to his store often to buy supplies and get their mail, and he told me last week that this isn't over. He said, 'I'm not sayin' they *did* or *didn't* do it, but I do know that if these men are anything like Epps and Burns, they will never let it end until it is finished.'"

William looked at me with concern and continued, "They told Mr. Bennett that you're puttin' a hurtin' on their money, and you're leavin' 'em no choice but to stop you. They think your words are gonna cause a slave revolt. They think if men like them don't make an example of you to the other preachers, then others might start preachin' 'gainst slavery, too. They won't have it. I believe Mr. Bennett's right. *They're coming!*"

"What do you mean, '*They're* comin'?'" Malachi asked. "We all know what *they* look like. Let 'em come. We'll be havin' a little meetin' here in a couple days 'bout 'em. Care to stay and join us?"

"Thanks for your offer." William thought for a moment and nodded. "I told Martha I wasn't sure how long my trip might take, so I might just do that." William then looked at Joseph and asked, "So, what are you gonna do, Pastor?"

"Ya mean right now, William?"

"Well yes, sir."

"William, the Bible says, 'Be still and know that I am God.' Maybe I'll get some fishin' in . . . but I'll be still while I fish. You can catch more fish that way—and plantations owners, too. Wanna go with me?"

"Pastor, that sounds good."

"Great-Grandpa, what kind of a meetin' did ya have? Who showed up?"

"Dan, a better question would be, 'Who didn't?'"

23

Malachi sent out runners to announce our meeting. The day was a busy one! Several local men brought smoked turkeys and venison. Squash had come into season, and it was baked to perfection. The house was filled with the smell of freshly baked cornbread.

It was late afternoon when Malachi welcomed one old Choctaw. As he invited 'im in, he greeted me by name, but he didn't look familiar.

The Choctaw spoke English well. "Pastor, we heard that those *hatak haksi*, or as you say, bad men, dressed up like us."

I looked at him with confusion. "Friend, where do I know you from?"

"You did good for me, up on the Ouachita. When sick, you hunted *issi* for food. You saved life of wife, Ohoyo, when our didanawisgi did no good. I come to pay back."

Before I could respond, I heard another knock, and Malachi opened the door. An old Cherokee entered with a younger one and nodded to me, saying, "Osiyo."

I replied, "Ostu iga." We looked at each other, studying the lines and wrinkles that seemed to map out two lives filled with adventures and the cares of life. He finally spoke to me: "Pastor, we have come to help. The words you spoke changed my life and my Ageya's life. I was at the funeral when you buried your little girls, Ruth and Naomi. I stood far away with my brothers. This is my grandson, Degotoga. I wanted 'im to meet you."

"Siyo, Degotoga. What does your name mean?"

"Sir, it means *standing together*." The young man moved closer to his grandfather.

I was filled with humility. "I thought so. That's what we need today." Elvy offered them some food, which they gladly ate.

I was sittin' at the end of the table when three more people entered the room. Malachi spoke to each of 'em as they made their way over to the table saying.

"Pastor, we're printers, and we're here to lend a hand!"

Another man in the room wrinkled up his forehead and quickly asked, "Printers of what?"

No one responded until finally one spoke to me. "I know he knows what we print, and Pastor, you probably don't remember, this, but before I got into *this* trade, I came to you when we needed food for our children. You went out to your corn crib and got some vegetables, a barrel of molasses, browned flour, and you gave us milk from your Jersey cow. I've never forgotten! This here is my son, Joseph. I named 'im after you."

I watched all those people fill the room. William was sittin' right next to me as I watched the wonderment on his face. There were many older men and even a few younger ones. Each came and introduced himself to me. Of great interest to me and others was a man who walked with a cane and had long, greyish hair tied back with a piece of rope. He walked slowly toward me with measured steps. He looked me straight in the eyes and said, "Reckon we're about the same age, and not sure what I can do to assist, but I'm here 'cause of a friend of yours and mine I knew down in N'Orleans back when I sailed with Jean Lafitte. He talked good things 'bout you and said he'd come runnin' if ya ever needed 'im. Preacher, Jim Bowie respected ya. He can't come runnin' with that big knife now, since the Alamo, but I can be here for 'im."

Malachi said, "I'm sure we can use you. "Always admired Lafitte after he helped General Jackson defeat those Brits in the Battle of N'Orleans."

"I was there!" The old pirate smiled a toothless grin. "And you're right,

General Jackson did help us give 'em there Redcoats a good whippin'. I know these bayouques like the back of my hand and every alligator by name. My boots are made from a alligator that tried to have me for supper." He limped over to the bench, sat down, and ate some pipin'-hot filé gumbo.

They kept comin' in. Each time the door opened, I wondered which chapter from my life would walk through it.

Then, some rough-lookin' cowhands lumbered in. They had guns on their hips, and they looked like they could whip a black bear with a switch. Malachi spoke quietly to 'em and then brought 'em over to talk.

The roughest-lookin' one, with black, curly hair and a scar on his left cheek, asked, "Preacher, do you remember me?"

"My eyes are not what they used to be, my memory neither. I've got sometimer's disease: sometimes I can remember, and sometimes I can't."

"When my little girl was real sick, you came and prayed for her on your knees by her sick bed, and she got well."

The other added, "My son died of the yellow fever, and times were hard. We had no money to bury my boy, and we were hungry. You took care of everything and then invited us into your home and fed us. It didn't matter to you that I was an outcast. You treated me and my family with kindness. You never condemned us."

Dan, I did not have the words.

Young Dan noticed tears in his great-grandfather's eyes. He went over and put his arms around him and said, "Great-Grandpa, don't cry."

Joseph wiped his eyes, smiled, composed himself, and said, "It was not me, but all Him."

Dan waited and then asked, "How many people came to the meetin' that night?"

"I reckon 'bout fifteen or so at first. It was interestin' to see all those folks in the same place at the same time and hear 'em talkin' amongst themselves."

"What did ya'll talk about?"

"Dan, it wasn't the price of cotton. If I remember right, there were lots of ideas bein' kicked 'round. Everyone had his own thoughts 'bout when and how Epps and Burns would appear again. No one believed it would be 'em in person that would come, though. One of the cowhands spoke up: 'This ain't no Bayou Boeuf, Cheneyville, or Bayou Chicot. This here's No-Man's-Land. Neither of those scoundrels would be crazy enough to show their faces here.'

"Another asked, 'What if they hire someone like last time? There's a lot of white trash 'round those plantations now.'

"I finally stood and spoke to the group, which had now grown to about thirty. 'Gentlemen, I want to tell you a story about a fourth Man in a fire. . . . ' Dan, I never get tired of that story. . . . remind me to tell it to you. I saw the worry slide off a few of their faces, but far from all of 'em."

"Great-Grandpa, you had thirty people to protect you?"

Joseph gave a hearty laugh.

"What's so funny?"

"Dan, that number multiplied like the fishes and loaves."

24

November 15, 1841
JOHNSON SWEAT'S HOME
TENMILE CREEK, LOUISIANA

One afternoon, about two weeks later, a worn-out gunslinger came ridin' up to the house. His mare was all lathered up, looking like he'd been ridden hard with no hay and put up wet. Malachi and I were sittin' on the front porch. He spoke urgently. "I need to find the preacher Joseph Willis. I have to speak with 'im."

"I'm he. Drag up a chair, and sit a spell."

"Oh, thank goodness. I've been ridin' hard from Nacogdoches to warn you there are three outlaws on their way to harm you.' So I asked, 'Son, what's your involvement with 'em?' He answered, 'Preacher, I met 'em two years ago in San Augustine County, Texas, during the Regulator-Moderator War. I was hired by one of the Moderators, Edward Merchant. The three of 'em were workin' for the Regulators Charles Jackson and Charles Moorman. The feud is still ragin'. Vigilantism is the only form of justice, so our kind of work is in high demand. I left Louisiana to make a better livin' in East Texas."

"Son, I know well about that feud. The roots of it began here in No-Man's-Land, with fraud and land swindlin'. I met Charles Jackson once in Natchez when he was a Mississippi riverboat captain. He's a fugitive from Louisiana justice now. I hear tell he shot a man named Joseph Goodbread last year and then organized the Regulators to prevent cattle rustling.'

The rider responded, "That's the pot callin' the kettle black. The news out of Texas is that the hostilities escalated four months ago, at Jackson's trial."

"Anyway, son, what does all that have to do with me?"

With narrowing eyes he informed us, "A man by the name of Epps hired these three outlaw assassins. They're 'bout two days' ride behind me. You need to be ready for 'em. They're good with their guns. They're a bad lot . . . been known to shoot men in the back."

I shook my head and spoke quietly. "Son, you're the fourth messenger."

"Sorry, Preacher, I don't understand."

"The first was an Acadian gentleman named Cormier, from down Vermilionville way, who gave me a warnin' to flee from a mob that wished to end my preachin' in a permanent way. The second was Malachi here, who warned me several years ago to flee from those who wanted to rob me of the few meager coins I had while I was sojourning here in No-Man's-Land. The third was my friend William Prince Ford, who gave me a warnin' just a few weeks ago, and now you appear like the fourth man in the fire. God has been good to save me from the evil plans of others. I have not even had the smell of smoke on me. Thank you for comin' . . . pardon me, I didn't get your name."

"Theo Cormier, sir. You said you had a friend in Vermilionville named Cormier? What was his Christian name?"

"Jacques. Jacques Cormier."

Theo's mouth dropped. "Pastor, he was my grand-pappy. *You* knew my grandfather?" There was not a sound to be heard for every bit of a minute. 'Pastor Willis, now I know who *you* are. My grandfather spoke of you often. You're the Apostle to the Opelousas. You're the Barefoot Preacher he spoke of."

"Great-Grandpa, ya mean the man that warned ya the mob was comin' and helped ya run off without your shoes—that was his grandfather?"

"Yes, son, imagine that! God had brought all this full circle."

"How'd Mr. Cormier know about Mr. Epps's plot?"

"Dan, once Epps got to Nacogdoches, that's where Theo's story began."

❧ ❧ ❧

Epps rode into town, and it looked like he had been ridin' for quite a spell. When he put up his horse, he asked an old timer at the livery stable, "If a fella was lookin' for someone good with a gun, where might he go to find 'im?"

"The Dirty Dog Saloon is your best bet."

"And who might he ask for?"

"That's easy. Theo Cormier. He's the fastest with a gun, and he packs a big knife, too. He's proved his skills time and time again but is an affable fellow."

Epps left his horse and went into the saloon, where he asked the bartender, "Where can I find Theo Cormier?"

Bartender tilted his chin and pointed. "He's sittin' over there playin' poker. Can't miss 'im. He's the one with the Bowie knife on his belt."

Epps approached him. "Excuse me, might we speak in private?"

"Let me finish playin' this hand . . . I never have much luck at this game." He smiled as he gathered up a huge stack of money, gladly folded, and gave up his chair. Theo asked Epps, "How can I help you, stranger?"

"Can we talk in private?"

They moved over to a table on the far side. Epps introduced himself. "My name is Edwin Epps, and I've got a job for a man with your skills."

"What kind of job?"

"I have a problem, and I need someone to take care of this here . . . umm . . . problem for me. Heard you were pretty good at what you do."

"Rumor has it I'm the best with a deck of cards 'round these parts. That *is* what you're talkin' 'bout, isn't it? Does this *problem* carry a gun?"

"Nope, he don't carry a gun at all." Epps moved to the edge of his wooden chair. "Look, I'm willin' to pay ya good money to take care of this for me."

"What's your problem's name?"

"His name is Joseph Willis."

Theo scowled and got a strange feelin' in the pit of his stomach. "You mean the Louisiana preacher, Joseph Willis? The preacher friend of Jim Bowie?"

Now it was Epps's turn to look confused. "Yes, they were friends."

He spoke sternly to Epps and shook his head. "Ya got the wrong card player, mister. I ain't gonna take care of no pastor problem."

Epps tried to back pedal. "Oh, Mr. Cormier, I didn't mean to kill 'em. I just wanted you to scare 'im."

"Sure, and you're gonna pay a lot of money just to scare somebody! Ain't no scary folks in Louisiana you can hire?"

Epps began sweatin' as he tried to clean up his newest mess. "Hey, you ain't gonna tell the pastor about this, are ya?"

"Epps, I ain't got no dog in this here fight. I don't know 'im. Never met 'im."

He went back to his poker game but kept one eye on Epps.

Epps walked up to the bar. The bartender had seen him with Theo and asked, "You and Cormier friends?"

"Old friends. I had some work for 'im, but unfortunately he's busy. You know someone else who might be in the same line of work as Cormier?"

"Well, I know some *hombres* that might. Not as good as Theo, but they'd probably help ya. They're a couple of Mexicans." Epps looked around to find 'em. The bartender just laughed and said, "Don't serve their kind here. They're down at Los Cuchos. Be careful down there! Lots of crazy fights over nothin'." The bartender laughed again. "Go on down there, and you'll find the brothers, Fernando and Julio, drinkin' mescal no doubt."

Theo later found out that Epps went and talked to 'em and told 'em what he wanted. They listened carefully, scowled, and threw their coins on the bar, sayin', "We dun't keel no padres!" He had no choice but to leave as Julio and Fernando gave him the evil eye. He turned to walk away and heard one brother say, "*Brujerio! Muy malo.*"

Then Epps went back to the livery stable to talk to the old man and get another suggestion. "You said Cormier was the best, but who is second best? I've been down to that Mexican cantina, and that didn't work either."

The old man played with his grey mustache and smirked. "Who sent you to that cantina?" "Bartender."

"Ya could've been killed there for blinkin' an eye. You're a lucky man. I know another one with two bad friends in the same line of work as Cormier, but without his scruples, and they're here in town today. They're good with a gun. They're just plain ole no-good cowpunchers that made a name in the Regulator-Moderator War. Go back to the Dirty Dog, and look for a bald headed, beady-eyed man named Scar Bartholomew, with two friends that are so ugly they'd scare a funeral up an alley. He wears a bull-hide hat most of the time. I hear tell he stole that bull."

Epps went back to the saloon and found the men standing at the bar. "It's been a long day, and it hasn't been a good one. Can I buy you and your friends a drink?"

They all nodded and one by one said to the bartender, "Make it a double of your best whiskey!" All of 'em sat down at a table, and Epps, by now no doubt feeling the effects of his brandy, told 'em his needs.

The leader shrugged his shoulders and said, "I'll do it for ya, but it's gonna cost ya. I get $3,000, and they each get $1,000 for this kinda job. We'll take care of this preacher-man problem for ya, but that's our preacher price."

"The deal was done, and the men were given half as down payment with the understandin' that they would get the balance in Alex when the deed was done.

The next day, as Epps's newly hired assassins were preparin' to head to Tenmile Creek, Theo walked into the stable.

"You guys takin' a trip?"

"Yup, we got us a nice job over in Tenmile Creek, Louisiana. Supposed to take care of some problem. The feud is a little slow this week, and *this* pays much better."

Theo nodded. "Heard the problem's a preacher."

They looked real nervous, and Scar asked, "How'd ya hear that?"

"Epps asked me first, but I turned 'im down. You boys watch yourselves in No-Man's-Land. It ain't no *Tejas*!"

They finished packin' and asked Theo, "You're from over that way. What's the best trail to take? We're thinkin' 'bout takin' the El Camino Real, then south along the Arroyo Hondo, and then over to Tenmile. What do you think?"

Theo smiled. "It'll do."

"See ya in a couple weeks, Cormier. No hard feelin's that we're not on the same side in the feud. Tell your boss we'll change sides if he'll pay us more.'

Somethin' about all this bothered Theo in his heart. He went back to his room and pulled out some old letters from Jim Bowie. He sat there and read one of 'em three or four times. In it, Bowie wrote 'bout how we'd thrown the devil preacher into the Red River . . . though I had only just *watched* 'im do it. Theo decided right then and there he should warn me. Any friend of Jim's was his friend, too.

He went to the stable, got his saddle horse, and asked the man at the livery stable for the quickest way to Tenmile. Wasn't long before Theo lit out on the Texas Road to Burrs Ferry on his way to Tenmile Creek.

He was told if he could find an old Choctaw trail north of here, it would make his trip even shorter. He started down an Indian trail but felt uncertain of his choice. He finally saw several Choctaws ridin' up ahead. They saw 'im, stopped, and circled 'im. Theo was concerned but spoke: "Do you speak any English or French? I'm 'fraid I might be gettin' lost. Can you help me? I'm in a hurry . . . I need to get to Tenmile Creek."

"Lookin' for a preacher named Joseph Willis?" They watched his movements very carefully.

Theo looked surprised but responded quickly, as time was slipping by. "Yes, I have important information for 'im. He's in danger!"

"We'll take you to 'im. He is a friend. We will trust the Great Spirit of the preacher to make journey safe."

"Thank that spirit!" Theo spoke under his breath, but there were a few who heard 'im and smiled. Theo and the Choctaw got to Tenmile two days ahead of the three outlaws. After Theo shared his story, Malachi asked the Choctaw, who had turned out to be a huntin' party, to warn everyone that I was in harm's way.

"Great-Grandpa, ya never told me a gunslinger from Texas rode all the way to Tenmile Creek to warn you that Mr. Epps's outlaw assassins were comin' to kill ya."

"Yup! I never told you 'bout their welcomin' party, either."

25

November 15, 1841
JOHNSON SWEAT'S HOME
TENMILE CREEK, LOUISIANA

Theo was exhausted after his long, hard trip and slept well that night. With the news that Malachi sent out the day before, people began showin' up by sunrise from as far as the Sabine and Red Rivers. In the mornin', I took a cup of hot tea Elvy had made and went out on the porch, I was sure surprised. The field was fillin' up with folks of all ages.

It was kind of excitin' to see all those people, but it was a little unsettlin', too! They just kept comin' from every direction. They carried guns, knives, and some even pitchforks.

Malachi walked out amongst the group and greeted 'em. It was early afternoon when he came back to talk to me about his plan. He had sent a few scouts out to send a warnin' of the outlaws' arrival. Malachi's plan was for everyone to come together just before dawn the next mornin' and for 'em to wait for the outlaws at the ferry crossin' on the Calcasieu.

"Don't you worry, Pastor," he said. "We're gonna take care of all of this for ya."

"I'm goin' with ya'll, Malachi," I insisted.

Malachi stared at me for a moment. "Pastor, can I talk ya out of that?"

"Not hardly! Remember that old paintin' in the inn where you gave me the warnin'? The one with Daniel in the lions' den."

"Yes, Pastor, I do remember."

"What was Daniel lookin at?"

"As I remember, Pastor, he was lookin' at the light."

"That's right, Malachi. He wasn't lookin' at the lions. Neither am I."

The next mornin' came quickly and quietly. I was somewhat shocked to see that a couple of women had joined the group since last night. I raised my eyebrows at their rather loud comradery. They were hangin' on a gentleman's arms. I recognized 'im from the Riverboat Rodoph on the Red River.

I gestured for the man to come over. He quickly came forward with his lady friends. Malachi asked 'im, "How long ya been here?"

"Just arrived from Alexandria. You were always kind to me, Pastor Willis, every time I saw you. No other preacher was . . . knowin' I'm a scamp who plays the cards and likes the ladies."

I was almost speechless. I had to ask, "Is that all I did?"

"That was a lot to me at the time, and besides, I can't stand Epps. He cheated me once in a gentleman's game of chance on the Riverboat Rodoph."

Malachi asked the gentleman, "Have you known your lady friends long?"

"Oh, no, I met 'em at a poker game. We had a bet on a single cut of the cards. High card wins. If I won, they had to come. As you can see, I won." With a wink, he added, "Forgot to tell ya, I had the honor of cuttin' the deck."

Malachi spoke to all of 'em. "Thanks for comin'." Malachi said under his breath as the three walked back into the crowd, "Preacher, is he one of your converts?"

I mumbled just loud enough for Malachi to hear, "God only knows."

Miss Elvy caught my attention, and I went over to her. She took my hand. I could feel her hands a-tremblin'.

"Pastor Joseph Willis, I know there's a lot goin' on right now, but I want you to know just how much I love you. I know I've fallen pitifully short on the obey thing, but there is no one that I respect and trust more."

"Miss Elvy, I love you, too." I could see that look of concern on her face.

"Are you worried about this here meetin'? Ya know, everything's gonna be all right. Their weapons will not prosper, nor can they."

"Yes, I believe that, but I could never forgive myself if I didn't say those words . . . especially if something goes wrong."

She put her head on my chest, and for a moment I just stood there and held her. I could see lots of stirrin' out there and could feel the stirrin' in our hearts, too. I thought, *Why does it take somethin' like this to get us to tell the one we love just how much we care?*

Excitement hung heavy in the air as a group of about two hundred men and a couple women started moving toward the Calcasieu in buggies and wagons, on horses and mules, and even some on foot. Malachi again, and now Theo, tried to persuade me not to go. Theo said, "Pastor, I don't think it's a good idea for you to go with us. It's just too dangerous. This kind of work is not for a preacher, not to mention your. . . ."

"Theo, I'm goin'! See Ole Sally standin' there like an oak? We once swam the mighty Mississippi together. We haven't lost but 'bout half a step since then." Ole Sally turned her head and gave me one of her looks. "Well . . . maybe a full step." She backed her ears and looked at him again. "All right ole girl, maybe two. But Theo, to me she's still a high-stepper—a real thoroughbred! And I'm just now gettin' into my prime."

Theo added, "Pastor, now I see why my grandpa admired you so much."

When the sun finally came up, it was amazin' to see all those determined faces. They were lined up deep and wide. It was 'bout mid-mornin' when the group reached about the halfway point to the ferry crossin', and one of the scouts came ridin' down the trail from the Calcasieu. "They'll be at the ferry in 'bout two hours, so you need to hurry. There's three of 'em armed to the teeth."

We reached the ferry just before the outlaws. The talkin' had stopped, and there was hardly a sound to be heard as they approached the ferry.

Theo came ridin' out to speak with 'em.

"Nice to see you 'gain, boys. What was it you said in Nacogdoches why you were headed here?" Scar hesitated for a moment, then said, "We're here to . . . to buy some cattle. You remember, don't ya? Theo, man, I had no idea you were headed to this neck of the woods, too. What are *you* doin' here? Who are all these people?"

"Oh, these are just a few of my preacher friend Joseph Willis's friends. We're here to hang some misguided cattlemen from Texas who are comin' to do him harm. I hear tell they're wanted in Texas, so the law's on our side, too. But, that doesn't matter here in No-Man's-Land. Here they just hang those kind and ask questions later."

The three men acted as if they'd just heard Ole Sally talk.

Theo continued, 'I reckon your cattle business is 'bout done here in Louisiana, ain't it?"

All of 'em shook their heads. "Yes, sir."

"Thought so! By the way, are ya comin' back to these parts to buy any more cattle in the future?"

"No. I think we're gonna buy 'em over in Waterloo, Texas, on the Shawnee Trail. You know the town, but I hear they changed the name to Austin two years ago. Prices are low for 'em there longhorns, and we hear tell they fetch good money in some parts."

"How do you know so much about the cattle business? I heard tell that you acquired some longhorns recently, for next to nothin' . . . more like free." Theo just stared at Scar and his friends. "Anyway, good to know ya don't got plans to come back this way again."

"None I can think of."

"Good choice. If ya ever have another hankerin' to come back *here* to buy cattle, I'll be seein' ya 'gain in Nacogdoches, and we'll be havin' a little talk *outside* the Dirty Dog about the high cost of Louisiana cows. Scar, ya got that?"

"I got it, Theo. When I was a little boy, you could slap the kid sittin' next to me in school, and I picked it up."

They turned their horses 'round and started to leave. Scar stopped and turned back. "That Joseph Willis must be quite a man, to have this many friends. I would like to meet 'em someday . . . but not on any cattle-buyin' trip."

❖ ❖ ❖

Before anyone could stop me, I gave Ole Sally a cue with my legs to move forward. "I'm Joseph Willis!"

"Well, I'll be!" He took his hat off and sat there a few moments, looking at the country preacher sittin' tall in the saddle while Ole Sally backed her ears as far as she could.

I wasted no time. "Are you ready to meet the Lord?"

"No, sir, why do you ask?"

"'Cause you came mighty close to meetin' Him today. I'll pray you'll have a safe trip back to Texas, young man, and that you get out of the cattle-buyin' business. Give my regards to Mr. Epps."

Scar put his hat back on, laughed, and rode off with the other two.

Then everyone went home. But, I had a chance to have a talk with Theo before he left. I found 'im later that afternoon, sittin' and talkin' to Malachi and Miss Elvy.

I suggested quietly to Theo, "How 'bout if we take a little walk down by Tenmile Creek? I'd like to talk to you about your grandfather."

"Sure, Preacher."

We walked down to the creek, and I asked, "Theo, do you know Jesus?"

"Pastor, my Grandpa said Jesus had bought my ticket to heaven. If I've been pardoned like he said, why should I do anything?"

"Theo, a dozen years ago in 1829, there was a man named George Wilson who was found guilty and given the death sentence for murder. But, Wilson had some friends who petitioned President Andrew Jackson for a pardon. Jackson granted the pardon, and it was brought to prison and given to Wilson. To everyone's surprise, Wilson said, 'I am going to hang.'

"There had never been a refusal to a pardon, so the courts didn't know what to do. The case went all the way to the Supreme Court, and Chief Justice John Marshall gave the ruling. I keep a copy of it in my wallet. Let me read to you what Marshall wrote: 'A pardon is a piece of paper, the value of which depends upon the acceptance by the person implicated. If he does not accept the pardon, then he must be executed.' God loves you, Theo, and yes, He has provided a pardon for you and me, paid for with Christ's own life-blood, but you have the right to refuse the pardon. Jesus was crucified between two thieves. One thief said yes to Jesus, but the other said no to Him. One accepted the pardon, and the other refused it. The question to you and me today is the same as it was 1,800 years ago: which thief on the cross are you? The one who said yes to Christ's pardon or the one that said no to His pardon? I have chosen to say yes. Theo, you have the same choice."

"Pastor, you have given me much to think about on my way back to Texas."

"Theo, I'm not going to talk to you as a preacher now, but as a friend of your grandfather's. I knew him real well. He was a good, honest man. I don't know how you got into this line of work, but I know he would want me to tell you to find some other way to make a livin'. This is not going to end well for you, and you have a good family name to pass on."

"I hear ya, Pastor, and I'll give it some thought. But, most preachers I've known just wanted my money, and I just can't stand those Christians that say one thing and do another. I once went to hear John Murrell, that man you and Jim Bowie threw overboard into the Red River. He said he loved Jesus and then stole my horse. That's why I came to warn you, after readin' Jim's letter about what you and Jim did to 'im. The French call people like Murrell an *ipocrite*. The English call 'em hypocrites. What do you call 'em, Preacher Willis?"

"Lost! Theo, there will come a day that you will meet Jesus. He will not ask you if you put your trust in Murrell, me, a church, religion, denomination, or any other person or -ism. He will ask you why you refused to put your trust in Him after He gave His life-blood for you. Ask yourself, how has He wronged you? How has He deceived you?"

Theo remained silent. I reached in my pocket, pulled out a Bible, and handed it to him. "I want you to read this. It will help you find your way."

He took the Bible, smiled, and said, "Just for you, I'm gonna put this in the inside pocket of my new coat . . . right over my heart. I'll keep it here, in honor of you and my grandpappy."

I didn't hear from Theo until I got a letter from him over two years later. Within a day, everyone had gone back home. For that one brief moment by His grace, God had let me see the fruits of my labor. But, Dan, every single apple, orange and all the other kinds of fruit from that tree came from the Vine, not the branch named Joseph.

⚜ ⚜ ⚜

"Great-Grandpa, did Mr. Epps and Mr. Burns ever have to pay for what they had done?"

"No, son. Not to any man, at least. They figured they might as well give up. They were hoppin' mad! They had each lost over a thousand dollars, plus the trust of many. Many stories spread throughout the plantations that Burns and Epps had some serious disagreements and angry words over what had happened. Epps was overheard telling Burns, 'Wish I'd never gone to that dat-gum feast of thanksgiving at Ford's plantation.'

"'Me, too. Ya kept nippin' that brandy from your saddlebags and ya got a loose tongue. Ya bragged about who ya were, how many slaves you owned, and your money. Ya should've kept your big mouth shut, but ya just couldn't do that, could ya?'

"Epps snarled at Burns. 'Well, at least I don't have the reputation of bein' the meanest plantation owner in Louisiana!'

"Burns fired back, 'At least they don't call me the "nigger-breaker"!' Their ugly words continued for several months. I heard that they have never spoken since."

"Great-Grandpa, to think all of that was over a feast of thanksgiving, too."

"Dan, Mr. Epps did not come after me ever again, but he certainly went after his slaves and my friend Solomon Northup with a vengeance. I think he was most cruel to 'im 'cause of our friendship."

"What did he do to Solomon?"

Joseph shivered as a cold chill shot through his body.

26

Dan, why do you want to hear all this?"

"I want to know about Solomon Northup. Is Mr. Epps really as evil as everyone says? What did he look like?"

"Dan, I'll tell ya all I've been told and seen, and then you can decide for yourself."

❖ ❖ ❖

Edwin Epps came to own Solomon in May of 1843. I don't know what the devil looks like, but Solomon described Epps as a very large, portly man with high cheekbones and a huge nose. I remember that he had cold blue eyes, thinnin' hair, and he stood a full six feet tall. Solomon also described 'im as repulsive, coarse, without manners, and clearly an uneducated man who used vulgarity whether sober or drunk. Epps is the cruelest man I know of, with the possible exception of his neighbor, Jim Burns. He's owned Solomon for the past nine years. I pray that ends soon.

I only met 'im two times. The first time was at Ezra's Bennett's store back in '27, when he was but a young man. I had stopped there on my way back from Mississippi after a little swim with Ole Sally in the mighty river. The only other time I met 'im was in '41, at William Prince Ford's feast of celebration.

I've only seen Solomon once since William sold 'em. It was on a trip back to Evergreen to preach at Bayou Rouge Baptist Church. After the service, Ole Sally and I traveled through Holmesville on our way to Bayou Chicot to preach a funeral. Little did I know that journey would take us right by Epps's plantation on Bayou Boeuf. After stoppin' to water Ole Sally in the bayou, there stood Solomon. I saw a couple of other slaves step out of the trees with heavy wooden collars 'round their necks.

As Solomon approached me I could see his scars from Epps's whip. I asked 'im what had happened. "What are all those bruises on your neck . . . and those cuts on your arms?"

"I'd rather not say, if you don't mind, sir."

"Solomon, I insist. Please, tell me how this happened."

"Well, sir . . . Master Epps got drunk 'bout a week ago. It was rainin' real hard. The thunder was crackin' every few seconds. We had all been sleepin' for several hours when he stormed in and started screamin' at us, 'Get up, you no-good, lazy niggers! You got some work to do.' He was so drunk that he slurred his words, but we still understood 'im. In his hand was his favorite whip, and he made it crack—almost as loud as the thunder. 'Get outside and line up. We're goin' for a ride.'

"I stepped up and asked if he wanted the team of horses made ready, but he just laughed at me and said, 'Get all the harnesses and bridles, and bring 'em to me.' Runnin' to the barn for fear of bein' whipped, I made quick time to meet all of Master Epps's demands.

"He began sortin' out all the tack and told us to get over to his carriage. He roped us together . . . got real mad when the horses' harnesses were too big for us. He then cracked his whip and told us we were gonna pull his carriage.

"There was so much mud that we could hardly get any footin'. Each time we slid or fell, we felt the lash of his whip. He screamed for us to go faster and got mad when we couldn't do it! He kept drinkin' and cussin' and crackin' that whip on us. This went on for a couple of hours, until Master Epps passed out in his covered carriage. We all went back to our cabins and tried to get dry. We heard 'im holler a few more times, and everybody froze, but he never came back into the cabins again that night ... except for Patsey's.'"

"Great-Grandpa, were there ever any happy times for Solomon?"

Joseph thought for a moment and smiled. "Yes, certainly he had some good times! He told others, and they told me about goin' to Christmas parties and other festivities at Madame Mary McCoy's Norwood Plantation. He called her 'the beauty and glory of Bayou Boeuf.'"

"Great-Grandpa, how'd a slave owner get a handle like that?"

"According to Solomon, bein' invited to Norwood Plantation was sure to be a time for great fun, savory food, and wonderful music. She was beloved by everyone. I met her at William Prince Ford's feast of thanksgivin'. Solomon also remembered a Christmas season when he was given leave to go and play his fiddle at one of her parties. He told others Madam McCoy was an angel of mercy who greeted everyone by name that walked through her front door with warm, friendly words and a jar of jam or jelly from her larder. She said, 'It's my little gift to sweeten your day.' That's the kind of woman Solomon described.

"Her guests were all slaves, and they sat at tables with fine linen and the best china. Accordin' to Solomon, there was plenty of food. Solomon loved her pies, cakes, and tortes made with her orchard fruits. She was so loved and respected that they actually brought her gifts of what they could afford."

"Great-Grandpa, whatever happened to Eliza?"

"Oh, Dan, after William Prince Ford sold her, Solomon told many that he heard that grief had gnawed a big hole in her heart. Her new master lashed and abused her unmercifully. She lost all her strength and wasn't even able to stand. She spent several weeks lying on the filthy floor of an old slave cabin. She was dependent upon the mercy of other slaves for food and water, but they were told not to enter the cabin for fear of the whip. One day, when the other hands returned from the field, they said that an Angel of the Lord had silently entered the cabin and taken her home to heaven."

"Great-Grandpa, how could anyone be that mean?"

Joseph bowed his head and studied the gnarled hands on his lap. "Son, I'm ninety-two years old, and I still don't understand that, either. That year was especially difficult for many." He lifted his head slowly and began to smile. "But, there was a better day comin': 1845 was the most special year in our family of both blessings and joy. And, as you know, it was a year of miracles."

27

D an, 1845 began with good news and celebration when your best friend, Julia Ann Graham, was born in February." Joseph gave him a wink and said, "Ya know, son, she just might make you a good wife someday. She comes from good stock—Robert and Ruth Graham from over on Barber Creek."

Dan's face blushed a bright red. "Aww, Great-Grandpa, she's only six years old. I tried to teach her how to fish. She was 'fraid to even put a worm on her hook, and she wouldn't help me clean 'em. All she would say was, 'Eww!'"

"I understand, Dan. Those are mighty important things—for a young man of your age." With a twinkle in his eye, Joseph said, "She probably can't cook, milk a cow, or saddle a mule, either. My eyesight has dimmed, and I thought she was your age, but son, it's never too soon to pray for the needs, protection, and salvation of your future bride, even though you might not even know her name yet. Who knows, the Lord may put a desire in her heart to like fishin' someday. Then again, He may not, but nevertheless she needs your prayers." Joseph dusted off his spectacles and continued: "I learned from my mother to pray for my children and children's children, as well as future generations of our family, and yes, my future bride, even though I did not know who she would be at the time."

"Great-Grandpa, what *else* happened in 1845 that made it such a year to remember for our family?"

"It was a year of new beginnin's. Life is a series of new beginnin's, Dan. After Julia Ann's birth, President Polk was sworn into office in March. We were blessed again with yet another addition to our family when your cousin Polk was born in June. Your great-uncle Lemuel named him James K. Polk Willis. I sure was glad when President Polk turned out to be a great president, or Lemuel would have had to change his name." Joseph laughed. "President Polk accomplished all he had promised to do, includin' annexin' Texas, which he did in '45, before the cholera killed him like it did my Hannah and Jim's wife, Ursula.

"But, just when I thought it couldn't get any better, your father was the first in our family to follow me into the ministry. What a day that was! Do you remember that Sunday, Dan?"

"Great-Grandpa, how could I forget? It was close to my sixth birthday, and Father and I celebrated together. There was only standin' room in the church, and all us kids had to sit on the hard floor. It was a very *long* mornin'. What I remember most was supper on the grounds after church. My father told me to stop eatin' so much, but I didn't listen 'cause everything tasted so good."

Joseph chuckled. "Dan, what I remember most was the look on your father's face durin' the service. He almost glowed, and his heart seemed 'bout to burst with love and gratitude. Don't know which of us was more thankful that day—me for havin' a family that loved the Lord, or your father finally surrenderin' to God's call.

"It was a year of change. 'Bout the same time as your father strapped on the sword of the Spirit, we Baptists broke apart over the slavery issue. In May of '45, we in the South split from our Northern brothers to form the Southern Baptist Convention. I could see it comin'. Louisiana Baptists have been splittin' over a lot less ever since. Some say it's cause we're autonomous. That may be true, but I tend to think some people's pride makes 'em think they got to have it their way, from the music to the hitchin' posts for the horses. There's a lot of chiefs and not enough of us Indians."

Joseph sat very still. He got a faraway look on his face, and it was one that Dan could not easily read. Finally, Dan asked, "Are you all right?"

⚜ ⚜ ⚜

Dan, I remember once in '45 when the Lord spoke to my heart while we were headin' home from church. Lemuel, Aimuewell, your father, and I were near Forest Hill. The Lord put it on my heart to stop the wagon and walk out to a farmer who was workin' a turnin' plough pulled by a team of oxen in the middle of a small field. He was all by himself—at least, that's what he thought. I poured him a cup from the water barrel on the side of our wagon and took it out to 'im.

The farmer told me, "You must be the angel I prayed for with that there water! I sure am thirsty."

I told 'im, "I'm no angel, mister, but I have news of livin' water, too."

"What kinda water is that, sir?"

"The kind that if you will drink of it, you'll never thirst 'gain." Then I shared the story of the Samaritan woman at the well as I took his hand.

He said, "I'm an outcast like her, mister. People call me a Redbone, and they sneer at me 'cause of my dark skin." I could feel his warm tears as they fell on our hands. We knelt in the red dirt together, surrounded by blown pine straw, and settled his future for eternity.

That red dirt reminded me of the scarlet thread that runs from Genesis to Revelation. Apart from Jesus' blood, there is no redemption, hope, or salvation. Those Louisiana golden pine needles reminded me of yet another thread. It, too, runs from the beginning to the end in God's Word. It is the golden thread of the Second Coming of our Lord Jesus Christ. It tells us that our Blessed Hope Jesus is comin' again. Soon, I hope.

But, it wasn't all unity in that year. In March of '45, William Prince Ford was excommunicated from Spring Hill Baptist. He was frequentin' too much with the Campbellites to suit the leaders there. Some said William was ordaining Campbellite preachers, too. When the good folks at Spring Hill got wind of it, they gave 'im the boot. Brothers Wright and Rand talked to 'im.

William told me Brother Rand said, "You were ordained to follow the tenants of the Baptist faith." Mr. Wright told William that he'd gotten off course. The conversation went downhill from there. I'm sure he knew it was gonna happen, but it caused a big stir from Forest Hill all the way over to Beulah Baptist in Cheneyville.

William asked me if I wanted my journal back. I told 'im, "Not hardly!" There were some who would not even speak to 'im or give 'em the time of day.

If that wasn't enough, Dan, I had to put Ole Sally out to pasture that year. She had been a good and faithful servant to this old hayseed preacher. We both knew she was way past the time that most mules would have just lain down and quit. But, like me, quittin' was not in her, so I had to make the decision for her. It was time to find her replacement, although I knew that was impossible.

I searched and searched, but couldn't find a one that looked like it might measure up to Ole Sally. Finally, I got the idea that I'd just let her choose. We went over to No-Man's-Land and found some printers of sort that I knew who also traded in mules. I put her in a pen with about a dozen others and just let her have her way. She did not take a likin' to any of 'em. When other molly mules came near her, she backed her ears and made some horrible brayin' sounds. She moved to the far end of the pen and after about half an hour, I went over and spoke in her ear: "Ole girl, I still have more travelin' to do before I go, and I can't walk it anymore, so I need your cooperation here. You know the Lord hates pride, Ole Sally, so help me out." She looked at me as if she understood every word I'd said.

She moved back toward the front and again backed her ears and brayed when the other mules came near. There was, however, this one John mule that trotted up to her. She looked at 'im and didn't back her ears.

I took that as a sign from Heaven and quickly made the deal before she changed her mind. I named him Bo. Don't ask me why. I suppose 'cause it was easy for me to remember.

He was more patient than Ole Sally but not as sure-footed. I never got the opportunity to see if he could swim the mighty Mississippi, thank God. He was more obstinate than Ole Sally, and that's sayin' something, but perhaps even a step or two faster. They both were smarter than a couple plantation owners I knew of, though.

❖   ❖   ❖

"Great-Grandpa, do you think that when I get to heaven, I might be able to ride Ole Sally?"

"If a lion can lie down with a lamb, then I 'spect you can climb on Ole Sally's back—that is, if she'll let ya. She might just tell ya—if she can talk like that donkey did to Balaam—that she's already laid down her burdens. But, Dan lets not get ahead of ourselves, she still got a few years left here. She's out to pasture, not dead. Now, son, speakin' of animals, how 'bout you go milk the cows and gather up the eggs from the hen house, too."

Dan was hesitant as he sat on the edge of his chair. "Great-Grandpa, please tell me just one more excitin' story that happened in 1845."

"You go and do your chores, and when you come back, I'll tell ya one you'll never forget."

28

Joseph had time to reflect on a very special time in his life, and when Dan returned, he was ready.

"Miss Elvy and I took a little trip to N'Orleans. I had been asked to speak at Half Moon Bluff Baptist Church, which is in Louisiana but on the eastern side of the Mississippi. I asked Miss Elvy to go with me, and she agreed, but only if we caught a riverboat at Baton Rouge after I preached at Half Moon and took a side trip to N'Orleans. She had our return trip all mapped out in her mind. I knew I didn't want to make this journey alone, so we left the boys with Lemuel's clan. She talked eagerly for several weeks ahead 'bout how we'd catch the Riverboat *Natchez* at Baton Rouge for our voyage.

"I hadn't been to Red Stick in a long time, and I'd never been to N'Orleans but Miss Elvy had seen the sights before. I remember how her eyes danced with the excitement of a child on Christmas mornin' when she saw all the lights and steamers. "Miss Elvy and I were both intrigued with watchin' the riverboats with their paddle wheels churnin' the muddy waters of the mighty Mississippi. There were lots of new riverboats from up north. An inventor named Fulton was mostly responsible for this boom when he took an interest in steam engines and started usin' 'em in boats. And, Jim Bowie and I never had cookin' like they now served. That night the bill of fare gave us a meal I won't soon forget. We both ate sauce piquante."

"Great-Grandpa, what else did you eat?"

"My mouth is startin' to water just thinkin' 'bout it. I had andouille and red beans and rice. For dessert, she had pecan pralines, and I devoured the warm bread puddin' with cream on it. We sat and talked for a long time as we sipped our steamin'-hot coffee. It was a delightful evenin', and we decided to stroll out on the deck. I still can remember the aroma of the jasmine and honeysuckle. We stood for a long time just lookin' over the riverbanks of the Big Muddy River. At dusk, a log floated by. Miss Elvy tugged on my shirt and pointed. 'What's that down there . . . on that log?'

"'I'd say that's an alligator snappin' turtle—the kind of turtle that can snap your finger off quicker than a duck jumps on a June bug.'

"'Looks kinda scary!' She kept her eyes focused on the black, spikey shell.

"We slowly came around a bend as we neared the Hamptons' House, the Crown Jewel of plantations in Louisiana with over 300,000 acres. Today, it's the largest producer of sugarcane in our entire country. But, it was the Houmas Indians who first owned the land. They should name it the Houmas House after 'em. Miss Elvy asked me if I'd like one of those. I told her I already have a mansion waitin' for me, but not built with human hands—slave or free. I reckon my corncrib in Heaven is bigger than that mansion."

❖　❖　❖

The many oil lamps and candles from the windows glistened on the river like hundreds of stars. It was light enough for Miss Elvy to see a tall building standin' apart on the grounds, and she asked me about it. I hesitantly told her, 'My dear, that is called a garçonnière. It is a house where bachelors entertain guests. I hear tell that is where some of the less honorable ones take female slaves at times. I told Miss Elvy, "My eyes don't see as well as they used to, so tell me 'bout all those other buildin's."

I heard hesitation in her voice as she said, "Looks like slave quarters."

I took her hand, and we walked to the back of the *Natchez*. She stopped and got the biggest smile. "Pastor Joseph Willis, didn't you promise to buy me one of these big plantations ... or was that one of my other suitors?" "Had to be one of the others, 'cause I'm sure I only could afford a mule and milk cow at the time. Come to think of it, I've not added much to my estate over the years."

Miss Elvy smiled sweetly. "Not much, you say? Not much except a place called home and nineteen children." We both laughed and talked 'bout what we'd been through in our eleven years together. We talked of how our love for each other had grown. Dan, love can fade at times, but what kept us together through the hills and valleys is trust and respect. It is what mattered most when our love seemed to flicker like the light of a candle.

We got up early the next mornin' as the mist was risin' off the water. We shared a pipin'-hot cup of coffee and watched the sun come up over the eastern banks of the river in N'Orleans. As we greeted the daybreak, we heard a most unusual sound. Miss Elvy's eyes got real big. "Joseph, what is makin' that hideous noise?"

"I do believe those are trumpeter swans," I told her as I looked over toward the edge of the river. We were comin' into the city, and there were some shallower little marshes along the banks. I motioned for Miss Elvy to come and see.

"They are the most beautiful birds I've ever seen," she told me. "By the way, how do you know about trumpeter swans, anyway?"

"When I was visitin' Jim Bowie once on the Mississippi, I saw plenty of 'em. Besides, I read an article by that artist James Audubon sayin' how they used to sell 'em in the markets here in N'Orleans. Sure are beautiful, aren't they? They say they mate for life."

As we got further into N'Orleans, there were many steamers comin' and goin'. The noise, sights, and smells were not to this here country preacher's likin', but Miss Elvy enjoyed every bit of it. I now knew how

Jonah felt in Nineveh, but I had a nicer whale to get me there.

We found an inn and checked in. I asked her what she wanted to do for the day, and she told me she was interested in seein' some fashion. Now, Dan, I sure can't say that was top on my list, but I wanted to make her happy, so I told her that would be all right if we could also see Jackson Square.

Miss Elvy commented, "I didn't know you were an admirer of President Andrew Jackson."

"Never said I was . . . I just want to see the statue of 'im."

Miss Elvy smiled and said, "Well, I declare, why?"

I told her it would be better if I just showed her. We took a carriage over to Jackson Square. I told her a most fascinatin' story about Micaela Almonester de Pontalba.

❧ ❧ ❧

"Great-Grandpa, who was she? That is a very long name, so she must've been somebody important."

"She was a baroness and *the* richest woman in N'Orleans. I told Miss Elvy how she got married when she was fifteen and went to Paris, but she was not in love with her husband. Her new father-in-law didn't like her and shot her four times in the chest, then ended his own life. She survived and went back to N'Orleans. Seems she made a visit to Washington, and President Jackson caught wind that she was in town and sent a buggy for her. She was a mighty independent woman. Kinda reminded me of Miss Elvy.

Miss Elvy quickly turned her eyes to mine. "Whatever do you mean, Joseph?"

"Oh, nothin'."

Dan, the baroness spent lots of money fixin' up Jackson Square. I heard tell that she used to go to the work sites wearin' men's trousers. The story goes that the President didn't like that and told her he wouldn't tip his hat to her if she continued to be seen in public wearin' pants. The baroness was a bit strong-willed and decided she'd have a statue built of President Jackson. You see, he's facin' her quarters as he tips his hat. I'd like to think of 'im today as tippin' his hat to my Cherokee people that he dishonored.

Miss Elvy smiled the biggest smile. We rode on in the carriage, taking in all the sights, until the driver slowed down, turned with a most unusual look on his face, and made the comment, "We are now comin' near the home of the voodoo queen, Marie Laveau. Heard she's havin' a two-for-one special today on love potions and pincushion dolls. Are you in the market today?"

"Not hardly. Please drive on!" Miss Elvy giggled like a little girl.

We stopped a little later for cafe au lait and some fresh beignets. I spent time with Miss Elvy in Vieux Carré, where she roamed through store after store and tried on many a dress. Then we walked back to the Victorian Inn in Vieux Carré.

Toward the end of '45, there were more joyous events. One would change our lives forever. There was also news from Theo!

29

June 1, 1844

PINTA TRAIL CROSSING ON THE GUADALUPE RIVER
THE HILL COUNTRY OF TEXAS

The sounds of change brought glorious news that blew like trumpets from Heaven. The first trumpet sounded with a story Theo Cormier shared with me in a letter.

A group of fifteen Texas Rangers rode out from their headquarters in San Antonio to look for a Comanche war party that was raidin' and terrorizin' the settlers. The Rangers traveled on the Pinta Trail as far as the Pedernales River without a trace of any Comanche. After nine days, the Rangers decided to turn back and make camp at a crossin' on the Guadalupe River. One Ranger saw a large band of Comanche after climbin' up a bee tree. "Must be a thousand of 'em!" he yelled. It was there that those fifteen rangers found what they'd been lookin' for . . . and then some.

Theo had ventured to San Antonio, lookin' for employment. A couple of German immigrants hired him as protection while they explored the Pedernales River for a place to start a settlement. They told Theo they wanted to name the town after Prince Frederick of Prussia. One wanted to call it Fritztown, and another suggested Fredericksburg. When they returned on the Pinta Trail, they heard the sound of guns bein' fired like never before. Theo figured there must have been a hundred or so firin' by the number of shots. He quickly discovered the number to be only fifteen.

Theo told the immigrants to wait for 'im down the trail. "I got to know what kind 'a guns they're usin'," he said. He managed to identify himself with the leader of the men and soon discovered they were Texas Rangers. Rememberin' our friend Jim Bowie, who had been a Ranger, Theo began to fire. The Ranger told 'em, 'Your gun will be of little effect again' 'em. Use one of my five-shooters!'

Those Indians started yellin' bad things in Spanish at the Rangers. They called 'em cowards and all sorts of things. The leader of the Rangers recognized the Comanche leader, Yellow Wolf. The Ranger finally stood up and hollered somethin' like this: "Yellow Dog, son of a dog-mother, the Comanche liver is white!" That's when the fightin' really began pickin' up. Theo thought, *Who is this man?*

Theo began to shoot and soon discovered he was no match with that Ranger. Within five minutes, Theo was hit with an arrow. It knocked 'im to the ground, and he lay there stunned. He lifted his head and could see the shaft of his demise stickin' straight up in the air. He asked himself, "Why ain't I dead?"

With a tremblin' hand, he reached inside his coat. There was no blood. As Theo sought to find his wound, he touched the hard Bible that was in the pocket of his coat. He thought, *I'll be! It would seem this little Book has saved my life!*

✤ ✤ ✤

"Great-Grandpa, was that the Bible *you* gave him?"

"Sure was! And when he opened it, the tip of that arrow's head stopped right on the verse talkin' 'bout how the thief on the cross asked the Lord, "Would You remember me when You enter Your kingdom?" That was the moment in Theo's life when everything changed forever."

Joseph added, "Theo said he made two decisions that day, one for Jesus, and the other to make sure he had one of those Colt Paterson rapid-fi-rin' revolvers. He said one Comanche who took part in the fight later complained that the Rangers 'had a shot for every finger on their hand.'"

"Great-Grandpa, who was the Ranger that gave Theo that gun?"

"I'm gettin' to that, Dan. Hold your horses. Theo told the Ranger, 'I've never seen anybody shoot like that. Who are you, sir?'

"'Hays, Captain John Coffee Hays, but my friends just call me Jack.'

"Theo also said that Hays's uncle was President Andrew Jackson, the same president who had my people driven from their land in North Carolina. Hays, who was also friends with Sam Houston, admired Jim Bowie and was a very brave man that day, so Theo decided to make an effort to be his friend. Hays moved to California in '49 durin' the Gold Rush, where he became the first sheriff of a place called San Francisco.

"Theo ended his letter with, 'One Riot, One Ranger. One Sinner, One Saviour. Theo.'"

30

Dan, 1845 was a time of plenty for Louisiana and our family. In November of that year, it was once again time for our annual feast of thanksgiving. I remember that a cool autumn breeze seemed to carry the excitement that was in the air across the scented pine planks here at Babb's Bridge to all our neighbors and friends. There was a hint of crispness in the piney woods that reminded us winter was just 'round the corner, but that Saturday was perfect in more ways than just the weather.

That day would change our lives forever.

There was nary a cloud in the sky, and the sun took care of the heavy dew on the pine straw as we set up tables and chairs. The smell of turkeys smokin' was just a hint of what was to come as far as the food was concerned. The place was alive with great anticipation as our family and friends began to arrive. Womenfolk were busy cookin' all kinds of Louisiana recipes. They'd been cookin' for days. There were sweet potatoes, okra, fresh-baked buttermilk biscuits, cornbread, butter beans, turnip greens with bacon, venison, hams with brown sugar glaze, and much more. My favorite pie kept callin' my name. You remember, Dan, the dewberry pie that Miss Elvy had made? We had plenty of coffee with chicory, too.

Mary McCoy from over Bayou Boeuf way brought a recipe with all the ingredients for a servant of hers to prepare. He served the many trays of French beignets covered with powdered sugar and some with fruit on top. They were kept hot in one of our brick ovens. I thought, *If I die today from eatin' too much, the French would have been able to do to me what they could not do in Vermilionville forty years before.*

We had so much to be grateful for that day . . . that year.

✣ ✣ ✣

"Great-Grandpa that was the best day of my life."

"Son, there *might* just be better ones. You still have a few more furrows to plough."

The family started comin' 'round mid-mornin'. Littl' Samuel and Aimuewell were of great help. Bein' eight and nine, they were responsible boys, and their mother kept 'em busy. There were probably four hundred people or so there throughout the day.

Our family mingled with friends, and everyone felt at home. Even Brother Robert Sawyer was there. He had been asked to leave the church a few months back for partakin' of ardent spirits and had promised never to touch another drop. He seemed to be havin' way too much fun for such an early hour. He was talkin' and makin' gestures to Malachi when I approached.

Malachi turned and quietly said, "Pastor, if I didn't know better, I'd say he was higher than a Louisiana pine."

I looked at Brother Sawyer and asked, "Have you been into somethin' stronger than the lemonade?"

"Oh no, Pastor. I tasted a little of the cookin' sherry that your sweet ladies were usin' up at the kitchen to make sure it had not gone bad. You know I don't partake of the devil's poison anymore, since Spring Hill Church put me on the straight and narrow path. I told 'em I'd sign a pledge with my own blood drawn from my veins if they'd let me back in."

I just shook my head and said, "Brother, these here Baptist woman don't use cookin' sherry. Most of 'em don't, that is. Some say otherwise."

He had a sheepish grin.

Malachi smiled and asked, "Is *he* another one of your converts, Pastor?"

"Yes, sir. At least that's what I hear he's been tellin' everyone from the Calcasieu to as far away as the Red River."

"I was most surprised and happy to see Theo come ridin' up in a one-horse buggy made for two. He had a young woman with 'im, and when he saw me, he jumped out of the wagon, leavin' his lady friend just sittin' there. The burly bear hug he gave me almost took my breath away, but it was wonderful to see 'im. I told 'im I got his letter and reminded 'im to attend to his guest.

He laughed and apologized to her as he helped her down. "Pastor, I'd like you to meet my fiancée, Adelaide Chevalier. She's from Baton Rouge by way of N'Orleans—and quite the cook."

"Theo, I can see you been eatin' a lot of her exquisite cookin', too!

"It is a pleasure to meet you, Miss Chevalier. I pray that the two of you will be very blessed together."

"Pastor, I wanted to thank you in person for your words down on Tenmile Creek. Although it took a Comanche's arrow a half-inch from my heart to change my heart."

Theo then told his entire story to the crowd that had gathered 'round, and when he had finished, everyone encouraged 'im. Theo also shared the story of their engagement with a much smaller group.

⚜ ⚜ ⚜

I went to Mr. Chevalier's home to ask for Adelaide's hand in marriage. We stood outside on the front steps to talk. He asked me, "Can ya feed her, Theo?"

I felt as poor as Job's turkey. "Mr. Chevalier, sir, I got a barrel of molasses, a barrel of corn, a milk cow, and a mule that can jump any object he can see over."

He replied, "My, you *are* richer than I was at your age, son."

"Sir, I love your daughter and would do anythin' for her."

"Oh, well, we will see. Are you a Christian, Theo?"

"Yes, sir, I am."

"Do ya believe the story of Jacob in the Bible is true?"

"Yes, sir, I do, Mr. Chevalier."

"You know Jacob had to work seven years for his wife. You willin' to work for me for seven years for my daughter?"

I didn't know what to say. All I could do was nod my head a little. Suddenly, there was a lot of laughin' goin' on inside the house. Mr. Chevalier thought it was quite funny, too, and said, "Son, you can have my blessin' *and* my daughter. She's been readin' 'bout those liberated women in Paris, so ya don't have to worry 'bout feedin' her, 'cause she can do that for herself now. At least, that's what she tells everyone who will listen."

Mr. Chevalier told me, "Adelaide is behind that wall listenin' to see just how much you love her." When Miss Adelaide came out, she was gigglin'. Mr. Chevalier explained that when his father-in-law asked 'im the same question, he tried to bargain 'im down to one year. I told Adelaide, 'I would have done the full seven years.

She said, "Sure you would have, Theo. *Sure.*" Then she smiled at me with a twinkle in her eye.

"Dan, while Theo was tellin' the story, the children were playin' tag and hide-and-go-seek. It was still warm enough that some of 'em braved the frigid waters of Spring Creek to take a final swim before winter. That was the final swim for everyone except you, Dan, 'cause *you* swim in it no matter what month it is. The rope swing got plenty of use that day.

"It was early afternoon when we finally sat down at the tables and some on the ground to enjoy our meal together. I looked 'round for William but did not see 'em anywhere. I had wanted 'im to give the blessin'. Instead, I asked your father to bless the food. We ate and talked through the entire meal." Joseph was quiet and stared off into the distance, lost in the moment. "Dan, what do you remember most 'bout that feast of thanksgivin'?"

"That's easy. That's the day that you gave me my very own lineback dun gelding. When my father lead Dollar out, he stood even taller than Bo. Great-Grandpa, as you would say, you made me happier than a coon in a hollow log."

Joseph rubbed the top of Dan's head and smiled. "You've turned into quite a cowhand, I hear tell, even better than most of 'em Texas boys."

"Great-Grandpa, I don't mean to say everythin' else wasn't wonderful that year, too. As you have said many times, 'What happened later at the feast of celebration put the ribbon and bow on 1845.' Will you tell me again that story? I want to hear it again."

As I remember Dan I wanted to close the celebration by introducin' all my children that were there—your grandfather Agerton, Mary, Joseph Jr., Rachel, Jemima, Sally, Sarah, William, Lemuel, John, Martha, Samuel, and Aimuewell.

Then I added, "And my surrogate son too, William Prince Ford. It would seem he could not make it today. He's been through a lot lately."

Then, you interjected from high on Dollar's back, "Great-Grandpa, I see Mr. Ford comin' this way in an open carriage."

Malachi was standin' right next to the table and hopped up on it. "Pastor, it is William, and it looks like he's got some folks with 'im."

"Malachi, my eyes are dim. Who's he got with 'im? Is it Martha and Peter? I so hope so!"

William had to leave his carriage far away in the field 'cause of all the other wagons, horses, and mules.

Malachi said, "Pastor, he seems to have three others with 'im. Looks like a nice-lookin' family: a woman in a lace bonnet with two well-dressed children."

I said, "I suppose they are Martha's people from Bayou Boeuf."

The closer they got, I could see that the woman was holdin' the hands of two children. William was walkin' in front of 'em and smilin'. I suddenly recognized the woman. "Eliza? Is it really you?"

"Yes, Pastor, and I want you to meet my children, Randall and Emily."

I looked up toward heaven and said, "Who is likened unto You, Lord?" I then bent down to Randall's eye level, shook his hand, and hugged Emily. "I'm pleased to meet you, Mr. Randall, Miss Emily."

They both smiled and said, "Thank you, sir."

Malachi told William, "You are the angel of the Lord that Solomon Northup spoke of that took Eliza away that afternoon."

"Great-Grandpa, how can we stop the third wind, the wind of war? What would Jesus have us do?

"If my people which are called by my name, shall . . . "

2 Chronicles 7:14

Epilogue

December 25, 1852

EXCERPTED FROM DANIEL HUBBARD WILLIS JR.'S DIARY

BABB'S BRIDGE, LOUISIANA

Great-Grandpa Joseph Willis relived much of his life in Louisiana on the wagon trip in October of 1852 from Evergreen to Babb's Bridge. He poured out his heart to us, and I discovered a joy in writin' and keepin' an account of all his stories.

Just when it seemed that no day in our family would ever top the 1845 Willis Feast of Thanksgiving... it did. It all begin the first time ever I saw a white Christmas, December 25, 1852, in Babb's Bridge, and the entire family was there. Each family member brought a decoration for our tree. The cedar was so big that we had to cut it down three times just to get it inside the door. There were strings of popcorn, wooden figures, sugared fruit, paper dolls cut out by the girls, gingerbread, and somebody even brought a bird's nest. We had ornaments that had meanings, too, like a pine tree, which symbolized eternity, pinecones that meant warmth, and a teapot that signified hospitality, which has always been taught by our family. There were candy canes with the Good Shepherd's crook, with white stripes for the purity of Jesus and his virgin birth and the bold red stripes for Christ's shed blood. At the top of the tree was the star of Bethlehem made from a quilt. And, the Christmas stockin's stuffed with nuts, candy, and fruit hung on every available nail.

I'll never forget the looks on my cousins', brothers', and sisters' faces. Dolls, books, tablets, pencils, wooden soldiers, and even a rockin' horse were unwrapped that happy morn. I got a new writin' tablet that I started using to write this.

Christmas Day started with a few flurries, and everyone ran out to see the snow. Mother taught us to make something I'd never eaten before—ice cream. She showed us how to add milk, cream, butter, and eggs with the snow in a pewter pot. She had read where President Thomas Jefferson had even made ice cream with split vanilla beans. Imagine that! Our traditional hot spiced cider warmed us from the cold. The smell of roasting chestnuts in Mama's cast-iron skillet in the fireplace brought back precious memories of Christmas past.

As the flakes began to fall steadily, more guests arrived, including Mr. Cormier and Miss Adelaide. She was with child, due in a few months. Mr. Cormier told Great-Grandpa, "If the baby is a boy, we are gonna name him Joseph." Great-Grandpa's face shone with an all-knowin' peace. You could hear the excitement in their voices as Mr. and Mrs. Cormier brushed the snow off.

Mr. Malachi Perkins, Miss Eliza, Randall, and Emily came in together. Mr. Perkins went right up to Great-Grandpa and gave him a hug, sayin', "Pastor, we consider ourselves engaged, but as you know by Louisiana law, we can't get married. We've fallen in love, and if it was legal, we'd be hitched already." He hesitated, then went on, "We so want to do what's right in the eyes of the Lord. I remember ya tellin' me how your mama and daddy had a clandestine weddin'. I don't want to bother ya on this special day, but would ya mind thinkin' 'bout it in a few days and lettin' us know if ya'd perform our weddin' ceremony?"

Great-Grandpa took all of two seconds, grinned, and said, "Ain't gotta think about it, Malachi. I'd be honored . . . if ya don't mind if I do the ceremony sittin' down. I'm a half-step slower than I used to be." Everybody laughed.

"Ya know, Pastor, ya could get in trouble for doin' it!"

"Yes, I know, but I'm ninety-four, and my race here is almost run. What are they gonna do, shoot me? They already tried that, when I was only knee-high to a grasshopper."

The entire room seemed to be filled with a sweet joy. We all cheered and clapped. Randall and Emily looked the happiest. Great-Grandpa motioned for me to come over and whispered in a voice real low, "Quite a few folks are named after me now. If you ever have a son, Dan, you should name him Randall, after Eliza's son. You can even nickname 'im Randy, if you so like. That way, our descendants will remember that miracle and share it with their children."

We watched the storm bringin' heavier snow, which seemed to be driven by a blue norther as our neighbors Mr. and Mrs. Robert Graham arrived. And yes, Julia Ann was with 'em. Great-Grandfather asked to be carried to the barn to talk to his aged four-legged friend, Ole Sally. He told her he had a gift for her—a mule blanket that all the Willis women had made. They had made a matchin' blanket for him, too.

I listened to 'im sweet-talk 'er in 'er ear. He thanked 'er for being a good friend and told 'er that he could never have done it without 'er. As Ole Sally leaned over the stall gate, Great-Grandpa kissed 'er on the nose. She backed 'er ears, and he laughed, sayin', "Aww, you know you like it."

We carried him back to the house, and then I asked him to share his annual Christmas story once again. Everyone gathered 'round the fireplace. He looked like he was doin' what he loved best.

The wind was blowing the snow so hard we didn't hear Mr. Ford arrive with Mr. and Mrs. Peter Tanner, the brother and sister-in-law of his late wife. Mr. Ford rushed through the door with a great big smile, sayin', "Looks like Solomon Northup will be freed on January 3rd. He's gonna be a free man!" Again, everyone clapped and cheered.

Great-Grandpa's heart was full of joy. Mine, too! He beamed as he said, "I don't see how a Christmas could get any better than this."

He'd started to tell the Christmas story when there was a knock at the door. I jumped up to answer the door. There stood a snow-covered, half-frozen woman in a green hooded cape. Her hair was all wet and matted. All of a sudden, I recognized her—and so did everyone else. There were a few gasps and then lots of hugs. Great-Grandpa couldn't see very well, as his eyes were dimmed by age. He asked, "Who's that? Who's here?"

She put her finger up to her lips to keep everyone silent. No one said a word as she went over to Great-Grandpa, hugged him, and said, "Merry Christmas, Pastor Joseph Willis. I love you with all my heart."

His eyes glistened as he pulled her to him and said, "I love you even more, Miss Elvy Willis. Welcome home! I've saved a place beside me for ya. You're just in time to hear my favorite Christmas story again.

"He was born in a little-known village. He was brought up in another community that people said nothing good would ever come out of. He worked with his hands in a carpenter shop until he was thirty, and then for three years, he traveled as a country preacher. He never wrote a book. He never held an office. He never commanded an army. He never owned a home. He never went to college. He never traveled more than a couple hundred miles from the place where he was born.

He was rejected by the religious folk of that day. While he was still a young man, the tide of popular opinion turned against him. One friend denied him. Another betrayed him. Many even hated him. He was turned over to his enemies. He went through the mockery of a trial and was then nailed to a notorious prisoner named Barabbas' cross between two thieves. His executors gambled for his only possession—his coat.

"Most of his friends had abandoned him by then. When he died, he was laid in a borrowed grave. Then, on the next Sunday mornin', he rose from the dead. As we look back across eighteen hundred years and examine the evidence and sum up his influence, we must conclude that all the armies that ever marched, all the ships that ever sailed, all the governments that ever sat, all the kings that ever reigned, and all the presidents that ever led combined have not had the influence on mankind that this one Country Preacher has had!"

Not a sound was heard 'til Great-Grandpa said, "Merry Christmas, everyone!

I got a stirrin' in my heart and started singin', "Joy to the world, the Lord is come!"

Great-Grandpa and Miss Elvy joined in: "Let earth receive her King; let every heart prepare Him room...." Finally, everyone was singin'. "And Heaven and nature sing, and Heaven and nature sing, and Heaven, and Heaven, and nature sing. Joy to the earth, the Savior reigns!"

Appendix A

THE STORY OF JOSEPH WILLIS

HIS BIOGRAPHY BY RANDY WILLIS

PREFACE

My family's story in America does not begin here. It begins in England in 1575. That year Nathaniel Willis was born, in Chettle, Dorsetshire, which is a county in South West England, on the English Channel coast. The county borders another county to the west that contains my deep Willis roots, Devonshire. Why would my ancestors leave their homeland, England, for an unknown land fraught with danger? The answer was religious persecution!

In 1620 a small group of Separatists would flee England via Plymouth Sound, situated between the mouths of the rivers Plym to the east and Tamar to the west, in the county of Devonshire. Besides fleeing religious persecution and searching for a place to worship, they wanted greater opportunities. The *Mayflower* was the aging ship that transported them. They sailed from Plymouth, on the southern coast of England, bound for the New World, seeking their new Plymouth. There were only 102 passengers and a crew of about thirty aboard the tiny 110' ship. They found their new home and named it Plymouth Colony. They became known as the Pilgrims. Five died during the voyage, and another forty-five of the

102 immigrants died the first winter. There, they signed the *Mayflower* Compact which established a rudimentary form of democracy.

Nathaniel later moved to London, where his son John Willis was born in 1606, only fourteen years before the historic Mayflower voyage. Fifteen years after that voyage, at age 29, John may have sailed for St. Christopher (a.k.a. St. Kitts) in the West Indies on April 3, 1635, on the ship *Paul* from Gravesend. But there is no record the ship stopped in New England. Gravesend is an ancient town in northwest Kent situated on the south bank of the Thames River near London. If the *Paul* was the ship John sailed on in route to the New World and carrying the dreams that would be passed on to subsequent generations, including myself, he may have barely escaped death. The Great Colonial Hurricane was in August of 1635. It was the most intense hurricane to hit New England since European colonization. If John would have sailed a month or two later he might not have made it to America, and this story, along with his dreams, would have ended at the bottom of the Atlantic Ocean.

Nevertheless, John Willis first appears in America in Plymouth Colony, Massachusetts, in 1635, when his son John Willis, Jr. was born. He appeared again in Duxbury, in 1637, when he married Elizabeth Hodgkins Palmer, on January 2, 1637. She was the widow of William Palmer, Jr. Duxbury was first settled in 1632 by people from Plymouth Colony, and set off from that town in 1637.

John Willis (a.k.a. Deacon John Willis), was later the first deacon in Plymouth Church. Reverend James Keith was the first settled minister in the area. The church parsonage, sometimes simply called the Keith House, was built for him. It is preserved and maintained by the Old Bridgewater Historical Society (OBHS), in West Bridgewater, Massachusetts. It is the oldest parsonage in America.

John also had brothers who were immigrants to the Plymouth Colony area. They were: Nathaniel Willis, Lawrence Willis, Jonathan Willis, and Francis Willis.

✤ ✤ ✤

The population was about 400 in the 1630s. John Willis would have known everyone in the Plymouth Colony area, especially its Governor, William Bradford, who was the English Separatist leader of the settlers there. William was Governor of Plymouth Colony when John arrived in 1635. John Willis held offices in Duxbury in 1637 and at Bridgewater in the 1650s. Bridgewater was created on June 3, 1656, from Duxbury, in Plymouth Colony. In 1648, John was a juror at the murder trial of Alice Bishope, who was hanged for killing her daughter, Martha Clarke.

In 1623, Governor William Bradford proclaimed November 29, as a time for pilgrims, along with their Native American friends, to gather and give thanks. His proclamation contained these words: "Thanksgiving to ye Almighty God for all His blessings." It would later be known as Thanksgiving.

A century later, John Willis's direct descendant, Joseph Willis, would marry a direct descendant of William Bradford, Rachel Bradford. I'm the 4th great-grandson of Joseph Willis and Rachel Bradford Willis.

✤ ✤ ✤

John and Elizabeth Willis had nine children: Sarah, John, Nathaniel, Jonathan, Comfort, Elizabeth, Joseph (1651-1703), Hannah, and Benjamin, Sr. John died August 31, 1693, in Plymouth Colony.

Benjamin Willis, Sr. was born in 1643, in Plymouth Colony, and died there, May 12, 1696. He married Susanna Whitman in 1681 in Bridgewater. Susanna Whitman was born in Devonshire. Benjamin, Sr. and Susanna Willis had six children: Abigail, Elizabeth, Susanna, Thomas, Benjamin, Jr., and Josie. Josie married John Council.

Benjamin Willis, Jr. was born in 1690 and died in 1779 in Bridgewater.

Benjamin, Jr. married Mary Leonard in 1719. Benjamin, Jr. and Mary
Willis had five children: Agerton, Daniel, Benjamin, III, George, and
Joanna. Joanna married James Council of Isle of Wight County, Virginia
in 1751. James was the son of John Council and Josie Willis Council,
and grandson of Hodges Council. Hodges emigrated from Devonshire.

Benjamin, Jr. and Mary Willis's five children would all move to North
Carolina. They would become the wealthiest plantation owners in Bladen
County, North Carolina, with vast land holdings, and many slaves.

One of these five children, Agerton Willis, and a Cherokee slave
would have a son. He was born in 1758. He was their only son. As the son
of a white man and a Cherokee, he lived as a slave on his own property.
He was cheated out of his inheritance by an uncle and rejected by many
in the family. He would fight for his freedom and change American
history. He was my fourth great-grandfather. This is his story. His name
was Joseph Willis.

HIS LEGACY

Joseph Willis preached the first Gospel sermon by an Evangelical west
of the Mississippi River.

He swam the mighty Mississippi River, riding a mule, into the Louisiana Territory before October 1, 1800, the date Napoleon secured the
Louisiana Territory from Spain. The Louisiana Territory extended from
the Mississippi River to the Rocky Mountains. The territory was vast
and largely unexplored, with many hidden and not-so-hidden dangers.

He was born a Cherokee slave to his own father. The obstacles intensi-
fied when his family took him to court to deprive him of his inheritance,
a battle that involved the state governor. Never daunted, he fought in the
Revolutionary War under the most colorful of all the American generals,
Francis Marion, "The Swamp Fox." He would soon cross the most hostile
country and enter a land under a foreign government, while the dreaded
Code Noir, the "Black Code," was in effect. In this territory, he preached

a message that put him in constant mortal danger. All of this was done under a cloud of racial and religious prejudice of the most dangerous kind. At first, his own denomination refused to ordain him because of his race. He lost three wives and several children in the wilderness, but he never wavered in his faith in Christ, nor in his calling to preach the Gospel of the Lord Jesus Christ.

MOVE TO NORTH CAROLINA

In the early 1750s, Joseph's father, uncles, and aunt moved to North Carolina.

The family traveled by sea, and landed down the coast at New Hanover (now named Wilmington), North Carolina. New Hanover had North Carolina's most navigable seaport, and even though it was not used much for transatlantic trade, this meant the area of the state was easily accessible from all other English settlements along the coast.

WEALTHY NORTH CAROLINA PLANTERS

On December 13, 1754, Agerton purchased 300 acres in New Hanover County (in what is now southeastern Pender County) "on the East Side of a Branch of Long Creek." Pender was not established until 1874. New Hanover included what is now Pender and parts of Brunswick County.

Agerton Willis was taxed on this property the next year, 1755. There were only 362 white people taxed in New Hanover that year. About twenty families owned a great number of slaves there during that time. These families, along with others like them in southeastern North Carolina, controlled the affairs of the counties in which they lived and set the standards of morals and religion. The four Willis brothers and their sister Joanna were part of this small, socially elite group of families.

Between 1755 and 1758, Agerton moved to Bladen County, just to the northeast of Daniel, Benjamin, and Joanna. Joanna's husband James had been living there since 1753.

It was in 1758 that Agerton's only son, Joseph Willis, was born. Joseph would someday play a trailblazing role in early Louisiana Baptist history and blaze a path for the Gospel of Jesus Christ that still burns today.

Most of the early Bladen County deeds before 1784 were lost due to a series of fires; thus, we are unable to find Agerton's first purchase of land in Bladen County. Nevertheless a description of the bulk of his lands can be gleaned from later deeds. He purchased 640 acres from his brother Daniel on May 21, 1762, on the west side of the Northwest Cape Fear River. He then purchased an additional 2,560 acres between October 1766, and May 1773, on both sides of the Northwest Cape Fear River near Goodman's Swamp. Altogether, Agerton's holdings formed a very large and nearly contiguous extent of land on both sides of the Northwest Cape Fear River, near the current Cumberland County line in present-day northwest Bladen County.

Agerton, Daniel, Benjamin, James, and Joanna were neighbors on the Northwest Cape Fear River. The other brother, George Willis, went first to New Hanover, obtaining a land grant on Widow Creek in 1761 and selling out in 1767. He then moved to Robeson County (formerly part of Bladen County), not far west of the rest of the family.

The four Willis brothers were all wealthy planters with large land holdings. As a planter, Agerton owned slaves, some of whom were Native American. At this time in North Carolina, many slaves were Native Americans; in fact, as late as the 1780s in North Carolina, a third of all slaves were Native Americans. Native Americans were made slaves by the white plantation owners from the very beginning.

William Moreau Goins, Ph.D., wrote in the educational *Teachers Guide South Carolina Indians* in an article entitled "The Forgotten Story of American Indian Slavery" that "When Americans think of slavery, our minds create images of Africans inhumanely crowded aboard ships plying the middle passage from Africa, or of blacks stooped to pick cotton in Southern fields. We don't conjure images of American Indians chained in coffles and marched to ports like Boston and Charleston, and then shipped to other ports in the Atlantic world. Yet Indian slavery and an Indian slave trade were ubiquitous in early America." Cherokee and other Native Americans were traded in slavery long before any arrived from Africa. The Indian slave traders of the Carolinas engaged in successful slaving among the Westo, the Tuscarora, the Yamasee, and the Cherokee.

BORN A SLAVE

It was to a Cherokee slave of Agerton's that his only son, Joseph, was born. The relationship of Agerton and Joseph's mother can only be speculation, but under the North Carolina laws of 1741, all interracial marriages were illegal. Since Joseph's mother was a slave, he was born to a slave status. It is clear from Agerton's will, though, that he did not consider Joseph a slave but a beloved son—in fact, his only son. This fact did not sit well with some other members of the family.

Agerton's will reveals he intended to free Joseph, but this presented legal problems. "An Act Concerning Servants and Slaves," the law in North Carolina, stated "That no Negro or Mulatto Slaves shall be set free, upon any Pretense whatsoever, except for meritorious Services, to be adjudged and allowed of by the County Court and License thereupon first had and obtained."

Joseph could not be freed solely by Agerton's wishes. In 1776, Agerton was only forty-nine but in poor health, and Joseph was still too young to prove "meritorious Services." Therefore, Agerton attempted to free him through his will written September 18, 1776, and also to bequeath to him most of his property. Just eighty days before this will was written, the Declaration of Independence had been signed, and times were very chaotic. Agerton would be dead within a year at age fifty.

THE RACE CARD

The problem for Joseph was that the family was advised by legal counsel that this part of the will could be overturned. This was a crafty legal maneuver by Joseph's uncle, Daniel Willis, for a slave could not legally inherit real estate at this time in North Carolina. Therefore, if Joseph was not freed, he could not be a legal heir. Since Agerton had no other children, this would make his eldest brother Daniel Willis "legal heir at law" under North Carolina laws of primogeniture in effect until 1784. Agerton had intended the trustee to obtain Joseph's freedom so he could obtain his inheritance, too, but Daniel ignored these wishes, as the following letter to the governor of North Carolina reveals:

Daniel Willis Senr. To Gov. Caswell Respecting Admtn. & C.
(From MS Records in Office of Secretary of State.)
"Oct. 10th 1777.
MAY IT PLEASE YOUR EXCELLENCY
I have a small favr. [sic] to beg if your Excellency will be pleased to grant it Viz. as my Decea'd [sic] Brother Agerton Willis gave the graitest [sic] Part of his Estate to his Molata [sic] boy Joseph and as he is a born slave & not set free Agreeable to Law my Brothers [sic] heirs are not satisfied that he shall have it. I am One of the Exectrs. [sic] and by Mr. M. Grice's Directions have the Estate in my possession as the Trustee Refused giving Security that the boy should have it when off [sic] Age If he Could Inherit it and now this seting [sic] of counsel some of them Intends to Apply for Administration as graitest [sic] Creditors [sic]. I am my Brothers [sic] heir at Law and if Administration is to be obtained I will apply myself Before the Rise of the Counsel and begg [sic] your Excellency will not grant it to any off [sic] them Untill [sic] I Come your Excellency's Compliance will graitly [sic] Oblige your most Obedient Humble Servt [sic] to Command

176

DAN. WILLIS, SEN.

Pray Excuse my freedm. [sic]"

The term "Molata [sic] boy" used by Daniel might indicate his attitude toward Joseph's mixed heritage, but I suspect he used it more for a legal emphasis on the laws of North Carolina in the letter, because virtually all Native Americans of mixed blood were known as mulattos in North Carolina at that time.

Later American history graphically illustrates the strong feelings of hate and prejudice toward Native Americans. More than seventy years after Joseph was born, President Andrew Jackson persuaded Congress in 1829 to pass a bill that ordered all Native American tribes of the South to be moved west of the Mississippi River. The Cherokees appealed to the Supreme Court, and Chief Justice John Marshall upheld their claim that there was no constitutional right to remove them from their ancestral lands. Jackson called this decision "too preposterous" and ignored the Supreme Court. He then ordered the army to "get them out." The Cherokees were driven out to Oklahoma on what came to be known as the Trail of Tears. Along the way, a quarter of them died. The Cherokees were one of the so-called Five Civilized Tribes and were the most advanced of all Native Americans, with their own road system and libraries before any white person came into contact with them. They considered all men to be brothers, yet this was of little importance to many of that day. No doubt young Joseph Willis would draw from these character traits from his mother, as much as he drew strength from his English father.

Daniel Willis's petition to the court also reveals that Joseph was not of legal age as of the date of the will, September 18, 1776. Legal age was then twenty-one; therefore, Joseph could not have been born before September 18, 1755, as some have supposed. It should also be pointed out that technically this case should have proceeded to the District Superior Court at Wilmington, but this court was in abeyance until 1778, following the collapse of the court law in November 1772. Therefore, Daniel was writing to the governor and council instead.

The Bladen County tax list of 1784 indicates that the case had been decided by then, since Agerton's property was taxed in that year under different family members' names. Even though Agerton's will had been probated and Joseph was living as if he were free, as he had always done, he was still technically a slave.

MY COUSIN'S KEEPER

In November of 1787, Joseph's first cousin John Willis, by then a member of the General Assembly of North Carolina and the eldest son of Daniel Willis, introduced a "bill to emancipate Joseph, a Mulatto Slave, the property of the Estate of Agerton Willis, late of Bladen, deceased." The bill passed its third reading on December 6, 1787, and Joseph was a free man by law at last.

The following quotes from the settlement listed in the final act are of interest:

"Whereas, Agerton Willis, late of Bladen County . . . did by his last will and testament devise to the said Joseph his freedom and emancipation, and did also give unto the said Joseph a considerable property, both real and personal: And whereas the executor and next of kin to the said Joseph did in pursuance of the said will take counsel thereon, and were well advised that the same could not by any means take effect, but would be of prejudice to the said slave and subject him still as property of the said Agerton Willis; whereupon the said executor and next of kin, together with the heirs of the said Agerton Willis, deceased, did cause a fair and equal distribution of the said estate, as well as do equity and justice in the said case to the said Joseph, as in pursuance of their natural love and affection to the said Agerton, and did resolve on the freedom of the said Joseph and to give an equal proportion of the said estate . . . Joseph Willis shall henceforward be entitled to all the rights and privileges of a free person of mixed blood: provided nevertheless, that this act shall not extend to enable the said Joseph by himself or attorney, or any other person in trust for him, in any manner to commence or prosecute any suit or suits for any other property but such as may be given him by this act. . . . "

There is a lot revealed in this document. First, note that they call themselves the "next of kin" to the said Joseph. The "fair and equal distribution" that is referred to turns out to be considerably less than the "graitest Part" [sic] mentioned in Daniel's letter ten years before. A later deed reveals that Joseph got 320 acres as settlement, and the above document indicates he also received some personal property as "consideration" for what "he may have acquired by his own industry."

The other real estate that Joseph should have received is described as "unbequeathed lands of Agerton" in later deeds, because this part of the will was overturned. These deeds reveal that Joseph should have received at least 2,490 acres, and other deeds are no doubt lost. There was also a vast amount of personal property that Joseph did not get. There was also an additional 970 acres deeded directly to other members of the family. Sadly, Agerton's will is lost, and this information is gleaned from other recorded documents and later deeds.

Joseph Willis could certainly relate to another Joseph, from the Bible, who later in his life would say, "They meant it for evil, but God meant it for good."

SLAVERY AND NATIVE AMERICANS IN NORTH CAROLINA

According to North Carolina genealogist and historian William Perry Johnson in a letter to Greene Strother, "In North Carolina, American Indians up until mid-1880s, were labeled Mulattos . . . " In her book, *North Carolina Indian Records*, Donna Spindel writes about the Native Americans of this area of the state: "The Lumbee Indians, most of whom reside in Robeson County, constitute the largest group of Indians in eastern

North Carolina. Although their exact origin is a complex matter, they are undoubtedly the descendants of several tribes that occupied eastern Carolina during the earliest days of white settlement. Living along the Pee Dee and Lumber rivers in present-day Robeson and adjacent counties, these Indians of mixed blood were officially designated as Lumbees by the General Assembly in 1956. Most of the Indians have Anglo-Saxon names, and they are generally designated as 'black' or 'mulatto' in nineteenth-century documents; for example, in the U.S. Censuses of 1850-1880, the designation for Lumbee families is usually 'mulatto.'"

Joseph's mother probably was not related to the Lumbee Native Americans. She was also not a part of the indigenous peoples of this part of North Carolina, since there were no Cherokees living in Bladen County at the time of Joseph's birth in 1758. Joseph's mother therefore would have had to have been brought to Bladen County, North Carolina, by Agerton in the early to mid-1750s or by someone else.

Tony Seybert writes in *Slavery and Native Americans in British North America and the United States: 1600 to 1865* that "Because of the higher transportation costs of bringing blacks from Africa, whites in the northern colonies sometimes preferred Indian slaves, especially Indian women and children, to blacks. Carolina actually exported as many or even more Indian slaves than it imported enslaved Africans prior to 1720."

NOTHING BUT A HORSE, BRIDLE AND SADDLE

Many years later in Louisiana, Joseph would tell his grandchildren, Polk Willis and Olive Willis, who were tending to him in his last days, that he left North Carolina "with nothing but a horse, bridle, and saddle." Polk and Olive later told their nephews John Houston Strother and Greene Strother this fact, and Greene Strother told me (also see Greene Strother's Unpublished Th.M. thesis *About Joseph Willis* and his book *The Kingdom Is Coming*). Different children and grandchildren also asked him from time to time about his heritage, and he would tell them his mother was Cherokee and his father was English, and that he was born in Bladen County, North Carolina. Family tradition is consistent among all the different branches of the family that I have traced and visited with starting in the 1970s. Every branch of the family, including some that have had no contact during the twentieth century, had this identical family tradition handed down.

After helping to emancipate Joseph, John Willis continued to have an incredible distinguished career. He became a member of the General Assembly of North Carolina in 1782, 1787, 1789, and 1791; of the senate in 1794; and of the House of Representatives in 1795. In the same year that he helped obtain Joseph's "legal freedom," 1787, he was appointed as one of a committee of five from North Carolina to ratify the Constitution of the United States. This was done just in time for North Carolina to enter the Union as the twelfth state and to assist in the election of George Washington as the first President of the United States.

In 1795, Governor Samuel Ashe commissioned John Willis as a Briga-dier General in the 4th Brigade of the Militia Continental Army. The land that the county seat of Robeson County, North Carolina (Lumberton), is located on was a donation from John's Red Bluff Plantation. A plaque remembering General John Willis stands there today. John Willis moved to Natchez, Mississippi, in about 1800 and died there on April 3, 1802. He is buried behind the Natchez Cathedral. His son, Thomas, later ran for and was almost elected Attorney General of Louisiana.

THE SWAMP FOX

It was during these trying times for Joseph that the Revolutionary War began in 1775. On June 14, 1775, the Continental Congress, convening in Philadelphia, established a Continental Army under the command of George Washington. Proclaiming that "all men are created equal" and endowed with "certain unalienable Rights," the Congress adopted the Declaration of Independence, drafted largely by Thomas Jefferson, on July 4, 1776.

Joseph and a friend of his from Bladen County, Ezekiel O'Quin, left for South Carolina to join up with General Francis Marion, the "Swamp Fox." Marion operated out of the swampy forest of the Pedee region in the lower part of South Carolina. His strategy was to surprise the enemy, cut their supply lines, kill their men, and release any American prisoners found. He and his men then retreated swiftly to the thick recesses of the deep swamps. They were very effective, and their fame was widespread.

They took great pride in themselves. Marion's orderly book states, "Every officer to provide himself with a blue coatee, faced and cuffed with scarlet cloth, and lined with scarlet; white buttons; and a white waistcoat and breeches . . . also, a cap and a black feather. . . . " Joseph would later proudly tell the family and friends, "We were called Marion men." The lessons learned with Marion would serve him well his entire life. Joseph was proud of his service under Marion, for at the time in Bladen County in 1777, it was estimated that two-thirds of the people were Tories. An oath of allegiance to the state was required at that time in North Carolina, and those refusing to take it were required to leave the state within sixty days.

Joseph Willis would not take this oath of allegiance, for he was a patriot loyal to his country, the United States of America. Loyalty was a trait Joseph Willis would display throughout his life—loyalty to his country, loyalty to his family, and loyalty to his Savior, Jesus Christ.

"Patriots" was the name often used to describe the colonists of the British Thirteen United Colonies who rebelled against British control during the American Revolution. Their leading figures declared the United States of America an independent nation in July 1776.

As a group, Patriots represented an array of social, economic, ethnic, and racial backgrounds. They included college students like Alexander Hamilton, planters like Thomas Jefferson and Joseph Willis's father and uncles, lawyers like John Adams, and just people who loved freedom, like 18-year-old Joseph Willis.

SOUTH CAROLINA

It was in South Carolina, with the Marion men, that Joseph would befriend Richard Curtis Jr. Curtis was to play a major role in Joseph's decision to go west. Later, in 1791, Curtis would become the first Baptist minister to establish a church in Mississippi. Ezekiel O'Quin would later follow Joseph to Louisiana as the second Baptist minister west of the Mississippi River in Louisiana. In 1786, part of Bladen County became Robeson County, and Ezekiel is listed as the head of a household there in 1790.

Early Louisiana author W. E. Paxton, in his book *A History of the Baptists of Louisiana, from the Earliest Times to the Present* (1888), would write many years later that Ezekiel was born in 1781, and every major author who followed used that date. Of course, this could not be true if he fought in the Revolutionary War and was a head of a household in 1790. Ezekiel's son John also wrote that Ezekiel "grew up in the same area as Joseph." Perhaps the Ezekiel listed in the 1790 census was his father.

JOSEPH WILLIS' WIFE RACHEL BRADFORD AND HER PILGRIM ANCESTORS

Soon after the Revolutionary War, Joseph would marry Rachel Bradford. Rachel was born in about 1762. Their first child, Agerton, named after Joseph's father, was born in about 1785. I'm a descendant of this son of Joseph Willis and Rachel Bradford Willis. Mary Willis was born next, in about 1787. Both of these children were born in North Carolina. Later Louisiana census records confirm North Carolina as their place of birth.

The last mention of Joseph in North Carolina was in the 1788 tax list of Bladen County. He was listed with 320 acres.

Taxed in the same district in 1784 was William Bradford, Rachel Bradford Willis' father. Rachel and her father descended from William Bradford (1590–1657). William Bradford had arrived in Plymouth in 1621 aboard the Mayflower, and on the death of the first governor of

Plymouth, John Carver, in the same year he was chosen as the leader of the Pilgrims and served as governor for over 30 years. William Bradford is credited as the first to proclaim what popular American culture now views as the first Thanksgiving.

The Pilgrims' story of seeking religious freedom has become a central theme of the history and culture of the United States. At an early age, William Bradford was attracted to the "primitive" congregational church in nearby Scrooby, England. He became a committed member of what was termed a "Separatist" church, since the church-members wanted to separate from the Church of England. By contrast, the Puritans wanted to purify the Church of England. The Separatists instead felt the Church was beyond redemption due to unbiblical doctrines and teachings. This Separatist view would greatly influence Joseph Willis over a century later.

By 1790, Joseph was living with Rachel in Cheraws County (now named Marlboro County), South Carolina, just southwest of Bladen County, across the state line. The 1790 census lists him as the head of the household with two females and one male over 16. In South Carolina, two more children were born to Joseph and Rachel: Joseph Willis Jr., born in about 1792, and Rachel's last child, named after her, Rachel Willis, born circa 1794.

It was also here that Rachel died in about 1794. She would have only been about 32 years old. Rachel may well have died in childbirth.

Joseph was industrious and prosperous. By 1794, Joseph had moved to Greenville County (the Washington Circuit Court District), South Carolina, and purchased 174 acres on the south side of the Reedy River on May 3, 1794. He purchased two adjoining tracts of 226 acres on August 16, 1794, and 200 acres on May 8, 1775, on the Reedy River. These three tracts totaled 600 acres. The 226 acres had rent houses and orchards on it. Joseph Willis, at this time, was well-to-do.

These deeds also give us the name of Joseph's second wife, "Sarah an Irish woman."

Two children were born in South Carolina to Joseph and Sarah: Jemima Willis in circa 1796, and Sarah's last child, named Sarah after her, in 1798 (she later married Nathaniel West). Sarah is called Joseph's wife in a deed dated August 8, 1799, but she died soon thereafter.

Joseph lost two wives in only six years. Forty-five years old and alone with five children, he decided to venture west into a land full of uncertainty and danger. He would sell everything and spend it all sharing the Gospel of Jesus Christ. He would deliberately place himself in harm's way to share this message. Personal tragedies, prejudice, and rejection by his father's family would have disheartened most men from their calling to preach Jesus.

BAPTIST BEGINNINGS

"Therefore, come out from them and be separate, says the Lord"
(2 Corinthians 6:17).

In Greenville County, South Carolina, Joseph joined the Main Saluda Church. He also attended the Bethel Association, the most influential Baptist Association in the "Carolina Back Country." He was a delegate from 1794 to 1796. Main Saluda was declared extinct by 1797, and Joseph became a member of the Head of Enoree Baptist Church. He was a member of Head of Enoree in 1797. These churches were rooted in the Separate Baptists, which sprang from the First Great Awakening. This revival, the First Great Awakening, would be a driving force that would greatly influence Joseph Willis's determination to carry the Gospel of Jesus Christ where no preacher of the Gospel had gone before.

Head of Enoree (known as Reedy River since 1841) was also a member of the Bethel Association. Joseph was listed in the Head of Enoree chronicles, along with William Thurston, as an "outstanding member." It was this same William Thurston who would buy Joseph's 600 acres for

$1,200 on August 8, 1799, after Joseph returned from a trip to Mississippi in 1798 with Richard Curtis Jr. It was also here at Head of Enoree that Joseph was first licensed to preach.

It is of interest to note that Richard Curtis Sr. was on a jury list in 1779 for the Cheraws District. This indicates that the Curtis family lived in this area for at least a short while. Other historians have also stated that the family was living in southern South Carolina at this time.

After a 1798 trip to Mississippi with Richard Curtis Jr., Joseph returned to South Carolina to move his family to the Louisiana Territory and sell his South Carolina property. Never one to squander time, he helped in incorporating the "Head of Enoree Baptist Society" in 1799 before leaving. It seems that he tarried until the spring of 1800 to depart on his second trip west, thereby avoiding the winter weather.

Joseph's Christian background was strongly influenced by the Separate Baptists in North Carolina and in South Carolina, although he came into contact with other influences in both states. The Bethel Association, prior to 1804, held in general Calvinistic sentiments. The majority of Baptists who entered the South Carolina back country, which included Greenville County, were at first known as Separates. Another member of the Bethel Association in 1797 was William Ford. Later, in Louisiana, Joseph was closely associated with a William Prince Ford and entrusted his diary to him. But, he was born in 1803.

An interesting side note is that just a few years before Joseph became a member at Head of Enoree, its pastor, Thomas Musick, was excommunicated in 1793 for immorality. This same man later organized Fee Fee Baptist Church in Missouri in 1807 (according to the church's history) located just across the Mississippi River near St. Louis. Fee Fee Baptist Church would be the oldest Baptist church west of the Mississippi River in the entire United States. Calvary Baptist Church at Bayou Chicot was not established until 1812. Nevertheless, Musick did not preach west of the Mississippi River until at least seven years after Joseph Willis did.

SPIRITUAL ROOTS AND THE FIRST GREAT AWAKENING

"Will you not revive us again, that your people may rejoice in you?"
(Psalm 85:6).

As a young man, Joseph heard and accepted the call to preach the Gospel of Jesus Christ. Joseph Willis's sermons were filled with the echoes of sermons and admonitions from First Great Awakening preachers like Jonathan Edwards, George Whitefield, and Shubal Stearns.

From 1734 to about 1750, the First Great Awakening ignited a fire for revival in the hearts of men called of God to preach the Gospel. The message of rejuvenation and life in the Spirit among churches that were stagnant, dying, or dead had an impact until the nineteenth century and the start of the Second Great Awakening. The results even can be seen today. In the late colonial period, most pastors merely read their sermons, which were theologically deep but lacked emotion and the call to repentance and salvation by grace through faith in Christ. Leaders of the Awakening, such as Jonathan Edwards and George Whitefield, had little interest in merely engaging parishioners' minds; they wanted to see evidence of true repentance and spiritual conversion. Colonists soon saw a change toward more animated and passionate preaching styles, encouraging them to claim the joy of salvation and to share the love of Christ through action.

Joseph Tracy, the minister and historian who gave this revival its name in his 1842 book *The Great Awakening*, even saw the First Great Awakening as a precursor to the American Revolution.

Whereas Jonathan Edwards sought to engage Native Americans, George Whitefield preached among the colonists. In 1745, Shubal Stearns heard Whitefield's cry for repentance and left the Congregationalist church. Stearns adopted the Great Awakening's New Light understanding of revival and conversion. This "new awareness" caused a division in the Congregational churches, into groups called Old Lights and New Lights. The New Lights claimed the religion of the Old Lights had grown soulless and formal—no longer having the light of scriptural inspiration.

The New Lights were zealous in evangelism and believed in heartfelt conversion. Sadly, by the end of the 1740s, many fervent New Lights concluded that it was impossible for them to reform established churches from within. Therefore, they felt the need to plant new churches to reach the lost and those who'd fallen away. Whitefield said, "Mere heathen morality, and not Jesus Christ, is preached in most of our churches."

In 1755, Shubal Stearns moved from Virginia to Sandy Creek, Guilford County, North Carolina, believing that the Spirit urged him to do so. Three years after Stearns's arrival and less than seventy miles from Sandy Creek, Joseph Willis made his entrance into the world.

In Paul's second letter to the Corinthian church he quoted, "Therefore go out from their midst and be separate from them, says the Lord. . . . " As Stearns and the other New Lights left the Congregationalist church, they became known as Separatists, using 2 Corinthians 6:17 as their guide. Eighteenth-century historian Morgan Edwards wrote of Stearns, "Stearns's message was always the simple gospel," which was "easily understood even by rude frontiersmen" particularly when the preacher himself felt overwhelmed with the importance of his subject. Most of the frontier people of North Carolina had never heard such doctrine or observed such earnest preaching. The Separatists had great missionary zeal and spread at a rapid pace to the other colonies.

Stearns and his followers ministered mainly to the English settlers, and seventeen years after Stearns's arrival, forty-two churches were established from Sandy Creek. Baptist historian David Benedict wrote in 1813, "As soon as the Separtists [sic] arrived, they built them a little meetinghouse, and these 16 persons formed themselves into a church, and chose Shubal Stearns for their pastor. . . . " Stearns remained pastor there until his death, and from this "meetinghouse" the South felt the flames of revival, the fan of which was carried west by an unlikely missionary named Joseph Willis. In 1772, Morgan Edwards wrote that Stearns's Sandy Creek church had "spread its branches westward as far as the great river Mississippi." After courageously fighting in the American Revolution with Francis Marion, "the Swamp Fox," Joseph Willis was the first missionary and church planter to preach the Gospel of Jesus Christ West of the Mississippi River.

MISSISSIPPI MISSIONARY

As mentioned before, Joseph was a member of Head of Enoree in 1797. Late that year or the next, he made his first trip to Mississippi with Richard Curtis Jr. This trip was made without his family, as it was the custom of the time to venture west, find a safe place, and then return for the family.

W. E. Paxton records the results of this first trip:

They sought not in vain, for soon after their return they were visited by William Thompson, who preached unto them the Gospel of our God: and on the first Saturday in October, 1798, came William Thompson, Richard Curtis, and Joseph Willis, who constituted them into a church, subject to the government of the Cole's Creek church, calling the newly constituted arm of Cole's Creek, "The Baptist Church on Buffaloe" [sic].

This church was located near Woodville, Mississippi, near the Mississippi River and due east of Bayou Chicot, Louisiana, where Joseph would organize his first church west of the Mississippi River, Calvary Baptist. Joseph returned for his family by 1799, but it would seem likely he might have made a trip across the river into Louisiana before this date, since this is where he returned with his family.

Curtis had already made one trip to this part of the country in 1780. In that year, Richard Curtis Jr., along with his parents, half-brother, three brothers, and all their wives, together with John Courtney and John Stampley and their wives, set out for Mississippi. Mississippi Baptist historian T. C. Schilling wrote that "two brothers by the name of Daniel and William Ogden and a man by the name of Perkins, with their families, most of whom were Baptists" were also along on this first trip. The late Dr. Greene Strother, maternal great-grandson of Joseph Willis and my cousin, told me that it was family tradition that Joseph's first trip into Louisiana was in search of a Willis Perkins. Years later in Louisiana (1833), a Willis Perkins was a member of Occupy Baptist Church while Joseph Willis was pastor there. According to Occupy Baptist Church minutes, another member of the church during that period was Greene Strother's father, John Strother. Joseph Willis, Willis Perkins, and John Strother attended the same church meetings at the same time. Census records reveal that this Willis Perkins would have had to be a son of the latter, though.

The Curtises were originally from Virginia. W. E. Paxton wrote: "The Curtises were known to be Marion men, and when not in active service, they were not permitted to enjoy the society of their families, but they were hunted like wild beasts from their hiding places in the swamps of Pedee." They were a thorn in the side of the British and their Tory neighbors."

Paxton continued:

They left South Carolina in the spring of 1780, traveling by land to the northeastern corner of Tennessee. There they built three flat boats, and when the Holston River reached sufficient depth toward the end of that year, they set out for the Natchez country of Mississippi by way of the Holston, Tennessee, Ohio, and Mississippi Rivers. Those mentioned above traveled on the first two boats; the names of those on the last boat are not known. Those in the last boat had contracted smallpox and were required to travel a few hundred yards behind the other two boats. Somewhere near the Clinch River, on a bend in the Tennessee River near the northwestern corner of Georgia, they were attacked by Cherokee Indians. The first two boats escaped, but the third boat was captured. The price paid for this attack was high, for the Indians contracted smallpox from them and many died.

Those on the first two boats continued on their voyage and landed safely at the mouth of Cole's Creek about 18 miles above Natchez by land. Here in this part of the state they lived. They called Richard Curtis Jr., who was licensed to preach in S. Carolina, as their preacher. He would later organize the first Baptist Church in Mississippi, in 1791, called Salem. As time passed the population increased. Some were Baptists, such as William Chaney from South Carolina and his son Bailey. A preacher from Georgia by the name of Harigail also arrived here and zealously denounced the "corruptions of Romanism." This, along with the conversion of a Spanish Catholic by the name of Stephen d'Alvoy, brought the wrath of the Spanish authorities. To make an example of d'Alvoy and Curtis, they decided to arrest them and send them to the silver mines in Mexico. Warned of this plan, d'Alvoy and Curtis and a man by the name of Bill Hamberlin fled to South Carolina, arriving in the fall of 1795. Harigail also escaped and fled this area."

Paxton said that the country between Mississippi and South Carolina was "then infested by hostile Indians." It seems likely that Joseph knew at least part of the Cherokee language, since he was half-Cherokee, an asset that could be of great help if the Cherokees were encountered again on the way to Mississippi. For this reason and, more importantly, because Joseph was a licensed Baptist preacher, that I believe Curtis brought Joseph Willis with him when he returned to Mississippi in 1798. Curtis was an ordained Baptist preacher also called to preach Jesus. In addition, Curtis knew well Joseph Willis's courage under fire, since both were Marion men together in the Revolutionary War.

After the trip with Curtis to Mississippi in 1798, Joseph returned to South Carolina for his family and to sell his property. As mentioned before, he sold all of his real estate to William Thurston in August of 1799, indicating his preparation to depart South Carolina.

The First Gospel Sermon Ever Preached by an Evangelical West of the Mississippi River

"Call to Me, and I will answer you, and show you great and mighty things, which you do not know" (Jeremiah 33:3).

When Joseph Willis crossed the mighty Mississippi River into the Louisiana Territory, the Code Noir, the "Black Code," ruled the Louisiana Territory. This decree from King Louis XIV regulated, among other things, the condition of slavery and the activities of free people of color. It also restricted religion to Roman Catholicism, forbidding the exercise of any other religion. The Black Code was in effect by law until the Louisiana Purchase on April 30, 1803. In reality, it was a hindrance to the preaching of the Gospel for many decades after the Louisiana Purchase. Joseph Willis would be hated because of his defiance of it. After crossing the mighty Mississippi, he would head first into the heartland of the Black Code, south Louisiana; that daring move would almost cost him his life.

In January 1797, the governing authorities issued regulations that made it mandatory for children of non-Catholic emigrant families to embrace Roman Catholicism and also forbade the coming of any ministers into the territory except Roman Catholics. Joseph Willis defied this most terrifying rule of law by traveling as far south as Lafayette, Louisiana, preaching the Gospel.

The exact date that Joseph preached in the Louisiana Territory west of the Mississippi River is not known, but what is known is it was almost three years before April 30, 1803, the date of the Louisiana Purchase, and in fact even before October 1, 1800, the date Napoleon secured Louisiana from Spain.

There are three facts that confirm the above statements. First, Joseph sold all his property in South Carolina in 1799 and is not found there in the 1800 census. Second, in 1813, historian David Benedict wrote in his book *A General History of the Baptist Denomination in America and Other Parts of the World*, "Joseph Willis . . . has done much for the cause, and spent a large fortune while engaged in the ministry, often at the hazard of his life, while the State belonged to the Spanish government." That would place Joseph Willis in Louisiana before October 1, 1800. Third, in 1854, the Louisiana Baptist Associational Committee wrote in Joseph Willis's obituary, "The Gospel was proclaimed by him in these regions before the American flag was hoisted here." That would have been before April 30, 1803. David Benedict was a contemporary of Joseph Willis and wrote his book only thirteen years after Joseph Willis preached west of the Mississippi River.

In violation of the Code Noir and at the risk of his life, Joseph Willis preached the Gospel west of the Mississippi even before Lewis and Clark began their historic journey by traveling up the Missouri River in May of 1804. He preached Jesus west of the Mississippi almost a decade before Abraham Lincoln was born. This would qualify as the first sermon ever preached by an evangelical minister west of the Mississippi River.

THE FIERY FURNACE

Joseph settled at Bayou Chicot between 1800 and 1805. In 1806, the Mississippi Baptist Association was organized. Though he was a licensed minister, a church had never ordained him. It was his belief that he should be ordained by the church. Some have questioned this and have asked why he did not just organize churches without his ordination. The answer is clear that he believed in the authority of the church and that it was important to him to be accountable to that authority, as he had been in both North Carolina and South Carolina.

He also knew well the importance of banding together with other believers, but there had been no need for ordination before, because the population at that time in Louisiana was very sparse—he had only six members in 1812 when he organized Calvary Baptist Church.

However, Louisiana was growing at a rapid pace. In 1812, the state population was slightly over 80,000. Eight years later, it was over 200,000, yet this section of the state was still thinly populated with churches twenty to fifty miles apart and having little communication with each other.

Therefore, in 1810, Joseph left for Mississippi to seek ordination. His son, Joseph Jr., would later often speak of Joseph Willis crossing the Mississippi River at Natchez and how dangerous it was. Joseph Jr. said that his father would swim the mighty river riding a mule in order to take a short cut and save time to preach Jesus.

After he reached Mississippi, once again the race card would be played. Joseph took his letter to a local church stating that he was a member in good standing while in South Carolina. The custom then as now among Baptists was to transfer church membership by a letter. The church to which he gave his letter objected to his ordination "lest the cause of Christ should suffer reproach from the humble social position of his servant." Paxton wrote, "Such obstacles would have daunted the zeal of any man engaged in a less holy cause." The "humble social position" of Joseph was certainly not his wealth but the fact that his skin was swarthy. I'm often reminded when I think of Joseph Willis at this point in his life of the statement that "the test of a man's character is what it takes to discourage him."

Once again, we see a very important personality trait of Joseph's that is recorded over and over again. He was longsuffering and willing to pay whatever price was necessary to proclaim the Gospel. After being betrayed by his father's family, losing two wives, and being rejected by his own denomination, he never became embittered. In Joseph's mind and heart, no price was too high for the cause of Christ. His focus was not on the fiery furnace but on the Fourth Man in the fire; he knew the safest place in life to be was in the fiery furnace, because that was where the Fourth Man was—his Savior and Lord Jesus.

Paxton wrote, "he was a simple-hearted Christian, glowing with the love of Jesus and an effective speaker." His youngest son Aimuewell Willis said before his own death in 1937, "the secret of my father's success was personal work." He said that as a boy he saw his father go to a man in the field, hold his hand, and witness to him until he surrendered to

Christ. Today, many generations later, his influence can still be seen. One grandchild said Joseph would be reading the Bible and talking to them as a few of them would slip away, and he would say, "Children, you can slip away from me, but not from God."

According to Paxton, "Joseph was never 'daunted,' for his was a high calling, a single-mindedness of purpose."

THE CHURCHES

After Joseph's rejection in Mississippi, a friendly minister advised him to obtain a recommendation from the people he worked among. This he did, and he presented it to the Mississippi Association. The association accepted the recommendation, ordained Joseph, and constituted a church called Calvary Baptist Church at Bayou Chicot, Louisiana, on November 13, 1812. Calvary Baptist Church is still active today and celebrated its 200th anniversary in 2012.

Louisiana had been a state barely seven months when Calvary Baptist was founded and was in a state of turmoil. Great Britain did not consider the Louisiana Purchase legally valid, and Congress had declared war on Great Britain the past June—The War of 1812.

Just a month and a day earlier on the Boque Chitto River, in what is now Washington Parish, Half Moon Bluff Baptist Church was organized. Located approximately eight miles from the Mississippi border, Half Moon Bluff was the first Baptist church organized in what is now Louisiana but was east of the Mississippi River. Some fifteen to twenty miles southwest of Half Moon Bluff Church, Mount Nebo Baptist Church was organized on January 31, 1813. Half Moon Bluff is extinct, but Mount Nebo is still active.

The Methodists had established a church even before these dates near Branch, Louisiana, but the first non-Catholic church in Louisiana was Christ Church in New Orleans. Its first service was held November 17, 1805, in the Cabildo, and it was predominantly Episcopal.

Paxton wrote, "The zeal of Father Willis, as he came to be called by the affectionate people among whom he labored, could not be bounded by the narrow limits of his own home, but he traveled far and wide." Once when he was traveling and preaching, he stayed at an Inn. There were several other men staying there, too. One of these men was sick, and Joseph read the Bible to him, prayed with him, and witnessed to him about Christ. The next morning all of the men were gone very early, except for the man who was sick. He told Joseph that the night before he had overheard the men talking about Joseph and that they had gone ahead to ambush him. He told him about another road to take, and Joseph's life was spared. Joseph would receive warnings other times, too, just in time to avoid harm's way.

Paxton said those who loved Joseph called him the "Apostle to the Opelousas" and "Father Willis." According to family tradition, strong determination and profound faith were his shields. He would often walk great distances to visit and preach to small groups. He rode logs in order to cross streams or travel downstream. He would sometimes return home from a mission tour as late as one o'clock in the morning and awaken his wife to prepare clothes so that he might leave again a few hours later.

By 1818, when Joseph and others founded the Louisiana Baptist Association at Cheneyville, he had been instrumental in founding all five charter member churches. They were Calvary, 1812; Beulah, 1816; Vermillion, 1817; Aimwell, 1817 (also called Debourn); and Plaquemine, 1817. Calvary was at Bayou Chicot, Beulah at Cheneyville, Vermillion at Lafayette, Aimwell about five miles southeast of Oberlin, and Plaquemine near Branch. In 1824, he helped establish Zion Hill Church at Beaver Dam along with William Wilborn and Isham Nettles. He went far and wide, establishing Antioch Primitive Baptist Church on October 21, 1827, just seventeen miles from Orange, Texas, and the Texas State line near Edgerly, Louisiana.

Joseph kept a diary. William Prince Ford arranged these notes in 1841, and Paxton copied them in 1858. Paxton admits most of his facts concerning Central Louisiana Baptists are from Joseph Willis's manuscript, which is lost today, and Louisiana Association Minutes. Ford also made remarks in this manuscript. Paxton records one of Ford's observations made in 1834, and it is very revealing concerning Joseph's heart:

Nearly all the churches now left in the association were gathered either directly or indirectly by the labors of Mr. Willis. Mr. Ford remarks of this effort: "It was truly affecting to hear him speak of them as his children and with all the affection of a father allude to some schisms and divisions that had arisen in the past and to warn them against the occurrence of anything of the kind in the future. But when he spoke of the fact that two or three of them had already become extinct, his voice failed and he was compelled to give utterance to his feelings by his tears; and surely the heart must have been hard that could not be melted by the manifestation of so much affection, for he wept not alone."

No church ever split while Joseph was its pastor. Baptist historian John T. Christian remarks in his book *A History of Baptists of Louisiana* (1923), "It must steadily be borne in mind that in no other state of the Union have Baptists been compelled to face such overwhelming odds; and such long and sustained opposition... The wonder is not that at first the Baptists made slow progress, but that they made any at all."

LOUISIANA PROPERTY AND SLAVES

The Opelousas Court House records that Joseph first bought land in Bayou Chicot in 1805. In Bayou Chicot, on June 29, 1809, he sold a slave to Hilaire Bordelon for $500.00. Again in June of 1810, he sold another slave for $480.00 to Godefrey Soileau. On January 5, 1816, he sold a slave for $200.00 to Cesar Hanchett, with the provision that this slave would be freed at the age of 32. On March 10, 1818, Joseph sold 411 acres for $2,000 to John Montgomery "in the neighborhood of Bayou Chicot." The deed reveals that Joseph had originally purchased this land from John Haye on September 21, 1809. This property had a great deal of improvements on it. On the same day, Joseph bought a slave from John Montgomery for $800.00.

Other deeds refer to property that Joseph bought while there, such as 148 acres he sold for $351.00 to James Murdock on January 6, 1824. This land was part of a tract Joseph originally purchased from Silas Fletcher on April 20, 1818. He sold the balance of these lands to Thomas Insall on October 31, 1827, for $500.

Joseph's last sale at Bayou Chicot was the sale of three slaves on August 17, 1829, to James Groves for $1,500.00. Thomas Insall paid off a note he owed Joseph on October 11, 1833. These are but a few of Joseph's business transactions while at Bayou Chicot. They confirm historian Benedict's statement in 1813 that Joseph "spent a large fortune while engaged in the ministry," for all of this money was gone in his later years.

It was at Bayou Chicot that most of his children were born to his third wife. The late Bayou Chicot historian Ms. Mabel Thompson of Ville Platte wrote me that she had in her possession the diary of her great-grandfather, who was the schoolteacher in that area. In his diary, he listed the patrons of the children who attended school. Ms. Thompson later mailed me a copy. Joseph Willis is listed as a patron on July 12, 1814.

According to Miss. Thompson in a another letter to me, "Chicot's chief attraction was it had an abundance of natural resources, such as timber, good water, wild game, good soil and friendly Indians ... Chicot became a trading center for a large territory extending as far west as the Sabine River, serving Indians, trappers, frontiersmen, homesteaders, as well as plantation owners."

THIRD AND FOURTH WIVES

Between 1799 and 1802, Joseph's second wife Sarah died. Joseph married a third time. This third wife was probably a Johnson and was born in South Carolina, but it would seem that Joseph met and married her in Mississippi or Louisiana. A son was born on January 6, 1804. He was named William Willis and is buried at Humble (formerly called Willis Flats) Cemetery next to the Bethel Baptist Church in Elizabeth, Louisiana.

Other children born to this union were Lemuel Willis, born circa 1812 (died 1862); John Willis, born circa 1814; Martha Willis, born April 9, 1825 (four females were listed in the 1830 census between the ages of five and twenty). There was also a Sally Willis listed in the 1850 Rapides Parish census as age forty-eight and living near William Willis.

The last two known children of Joseph were born to his fourth wife, Elvy Sweat. They were Samuel Willis, born circa 1836; and Aimuewell Willis, born May 1, 1837, and died September 9, 1937, at age 100. Joseph would have been about 79 years old when Aimuewell was born. The 1850 Rapides Parish Census also list an additional four males in Joseph Willis's household: James, born circa 1841; William, born circa 1845; Timothy, born circa 1847; and Bernard, born circa 1848. It would be unlikely that Joseph would have a second son named William. Aimuewell Willis always said he was Joseph Willis's youngest son. These last four males are most likely Joseph's grandchildren. Historian Ivan Wise wrote in *Footsteps of the Flock: or Origins of Louisiana Baptists* (1910) that two sons of Joseph died, "poisoned on honey and were buried a half mile from the present town of Oakdale, Louisiana."

Joseph's third wife died and is buried at Bayou Chicot. The location of her unmarked grave is unknown, but I suspect she is buried next to the site of the original Calvary Baptist Church, in Vandenburg Cemetery.

One historian wrote that Joseph Willis had 19 children. Joseph's children who were still living would follow him when he would later move to Rapides Parish. Many were neighbors with him as late as 1850, as the census reveals, as well as several grandchildren, who were grown by then.

Joseph's eldest child Agerton married Sophie Story, an Irish orphan brought from Tennessee by a Mr. Park, who then lived near Holmesville below Bunkie, Louisiana. Agerton's son, Daniel Hubbard Willis Sr., was the first of many descendants to follow Joseph into the ministry. Paxton calls Daniel "one of the most respected ministers in the Louisiana Association." He established many churches himself and was blind in his later years. His daughter would read the Scriptures for him as he would preach. He was pastor of Amiable and Spring Hill Baptist Churches for many years. He was my great-great-grandfather. He settled on Spring Creek, near Glenmora, at a community called Babb's Bridge. Many of my cousins still live in that area today.

Joseph's daughter Jemima Willis married William Dyer, and they lived on the Calcasieu River near Master's Creek. Mary married Thomas Dial (her first husband was a Johnson) from South Carolina, and they both were living in Rapides Parish in 1850. Joseph Willis Jr. married Jennie Coker at Bayou Chicot and later moved to Rapides Parish and settled near Tenmile Creek. Lemuel Willis married Emeline Perkins from Tenmile Creek and settled near Glenmora in Blanche, Louisiana; the late Dr. Greene Strother, Southern Baptist missionary emeritus to China and Malaysia, was his grandson. William married Rhoda Strother on the "Darbourn" on the upper reaches of the Calcasieu. Aimuewell married twice and settled in Leesville. His first wife was Marguerite Leuemche, and his second wife was Lucy Foshee.

Many of the descendants of these children live in these same areas today. At least eight generations have lived in the Forest Hill area, including Joseph himself. Oakdale, Louisiana, probably has more descendants of Joseph than any other area.

I visited with Aimuewell's daughter, Pearl, in Denver, Colorado, in December of 1980, and a short time later with Aimuewell's son Elzie Willis near Leesville, Louisiana. It was a strange feeling to talk with someone whose grandfather was born in 1758. Joseph was about 79 when their father was born, and Aimuewell was in his eighties when they were born.

No photograph exists of Joseph Willis. The photograph in Durham and Ramond's book, Baptist Builders in Louisiana (1934), is of Aimuewell, listed as Joseph in error.

IN SERVICE OF AMERICA

Not surprisingly, many descendants of Joseph Willis are Baptists, but far from all are. Many have fought in the major wars and served America faithfully. Joseph fought in the Revolutionary War. Daniel Willis Jr., Aimuewell Willis, William Willis, Crawford Willis (killed at Shiloh), and Lemuel Willis served in the Civil War for the South. Dr. Daniel Oscar Willis and Dr. Greene Strother served in World War I. Dr. Greene Strother, Joseph's great-grandson, captured more Germans than any other soldier, besides the famed Sgt. York, in World War I. He was awarded the French *Croix de Guerre,* the Distinguished Service Cross, and the Purple Heart.

Greene Strother also served as chaplain to General Claire Chennault's Flying Tigers while in China as a missionary. Like Strother, Chennault was reared in the Louisiana towns of Gilbert and Waterproof. A host of descendants of Joseph Willis fought in World War II, including Robert (Bobby) Kenneth Willis Jr, who was the first soldier killed in action in World War II from Rapides Parish, Louisiana. Louisiana's Pineville American Legion post was named in his honor (the post no longer exists). The Japanese killed him on December 7, 1941, during the surprise attack on Pearl Harbor. His body is entombed at the bottom of Pearl Harbor, aboard the *USS Arizona.* I have visited the *USS Arizona* memorial twice and have marveled at his sacrifice and the others as I viewed their names carved in marble at the memorial.

PIONEER CHURCH LIFE

After moving to Spring Creek, east of the Calcasieu River near Glenmora, Louisiana around 1828-1829, Joseph began to establish churches in that area as well. The first established was Amiable Baptist Church on September 6, 1828, near Glenmora. He next established Occupy Baptist Church in 1833 near Pitkin, and then he established Spring Hill Baptist Church in 1841, near Forest Hill.

Joseph was about 83 when Spring Hill was established. The Baptist churches of that day did not necessarily meet weekly. Preachers would have to travel long distances. Those who met weekly might have a preacher only once a month or every other month. Discipline was stern, with members being excluded (fellowship being withdrawn by the church) for gossiping, drinking too much, quarreling, dancing, using bad language, and in one case at Amiable, for "having abused her mother." But, the churches were also forgiving, if you admitted you were wrong and promised not to do it again. Repentance along with salvation was emphasized.

A good example is found in the Spring Hill Church minutes. After twice promising not to "partake of ardent spirits" any more, Robert Snoddy had the fellowship of the church withdrawn from him on May 31, 1851. A month later, Snoddy sent this letter to the church explaining his actions:

Dear Brethren, Having been overtaken in an error I set down to confess it. I did use liquor too freely, but did not say anything or do anything out of the way. In as much as I do expect to be at the conference I send you my thoughts. I did promise you that I would refrain from using the poison, but I having broken my promise I have therefore rendered myself unworthy of your fellowship and cannot murmur if you exclude me. I suppose it is no use to tell you that I have been sincerely punished for my crime in as much as I have confessed the same to you before, but I make this last request of you for forgiveness, or is your forgiveness exhausted towards me. It is necessary that I say to you that I sorely repented for my guilt, but my brethren if you have in your wisdom supposed that my life brings too much reproach on that most respectful of all causes, exclude me, exclude me, oh exclude me. But I do love the cause so well that I will try to be at the door of the temple of the Lord. Brethren, whilst you are dealing with me, do it mercifully, prayerfully, and candidly. I was presented by a beloved brother with a temperance pledge to which I replied I would think about it, but if I could have obtained enough of my heart's blood to fill my pen to write my name I would have done it. It is my determination to join it yet—and never taste another drop of the deathly cup whilst I live, at the peril of my life. Nothing more, but I request your prayers, dear brethren—Robert Snoddy

Robert Snoddy was restored to membership. Four months later, he was once again reported drinking and once again excluded.

The Amiable Baptist Church minutes in 1879 declared their position in no uncertain terms: "On motion be it resolved that we as a church are willing to look over and forgive the past, and we as a church for the time to come allow no more playing or dancing among our church members. If they do, they may expect to be dealt with." The Amiable minutes record that one dear member was admonished at a church service for dancing. He then stood in the church aisle, did a jig, and walked out.

Pastors were usually called to preach by the church for a one-year period. In 1857, Amiable voted to give Pastor D. H. Willis $100.00 "to sustain him for the next twelve months . . . it being the amount stated by him."

In 1833, Joseph became pastor of Occupy Baptist Church near Pitkin, Louisiana. The church is presently located next to Tenmile Creek. He served as pastor there for about 16 years. There he married Elvy Sweat, who was many years younger than he. She is listed as age 30 in the 1850 census; Joseph is listed as 98 in the same census. He was actually only a mere 92. I suspect her age is listed wrong too. Joseph's son Lemuel and others said she was not good to him. As a result of this and Joseph's failing health, his son Lemuel and two men went and got him. They took him to Lemuel's home in Blanche, Louisiana, where he lived the remainder of his life.

On a bed in an ox wagon used for an ambulance, he sang as the wagon rolled along to Lemuel's home. Joseph witnessed to the two men while lying in the back of the wagon. He preached to his last breath, either from a chair in the church or from his bed at home.

It was during this time that a man named John Phillips, from the government, came by taking affidavits as to the population's race. Joseph signed this affidavit and stated that his mother was Cherokee and his father was English. This was registered at the courthouse in Alexandria, Louisiana.

HOMECOMING IN HEAVEN

Joseph Willis died on September 14, 1854, in Blanche, Louisiana, about three miles south of Glenmora. He is buried in the Occupy Baptist Church cemetery. Twenty years after he began his ministry in Louisiana in 1800, there were only ten preachers and eight Baptist churches with a membership of 150 in the entire state. On January 18, 1955, just over 100 years after his death, 250 people, among them 16 ministers, gathered in freezing weather to unveil a monument in his memory at his grave.

The Louisiana Association published the following estimate of his work:

Before the church began to send missionaries into destitute regions, he at his own expense, and frequently at the risk of his life, came to these parts, preaching the gospel of the Redeemer. For fifty years he was instant in season and out of season, preaching, exhorting, and instructing regarding not his property, his health or even his life, if he might be the means of turning sinners to Christ.

Louisiana Baptist historian Glen Lee Greene wrote in *House Upon A Rock* (1973), "In all the history of Louisiana Baptists it would be difficult, if not impossible, to find a man who suffered more reverses, who enjoyed fewer rewards, or who single-handedly achieved more enduring results for the denomination than did Joseph Willis."

Appendix B

THE BIRTH OF THE NOVELS AND THE PLAY AND, THE REAL-LIFE CON-
NECTIONS BETWEEN WILLIAM PRINCE FORD, SOLOMON NORTHUP,
JIM BOWIE, AND JOSEPH WILLIS

A s a child Randy Willis lived near Longleaf and Forest Hill, Louisiana. As a teenager, he would work cows with his family there on
the open range, owned by lumber companies. Seven generations of his
family have lived there, beginning with his 4th great-grandfather—Joseph
Willis. He would often ride his horse through his family's neighboring
property, which was once William Prince Ford's Wallfield Plantation,
not realizing the significance of his ancestor's connection to Solomon
Northup and William Prince Ford.

⚜ ⚜ ⚜

After writing the biography *The Apostle to the Opelousas*, Randy Willis
got the idea for his novels *Twice a Slave* and *Three Winds Blowing* and the
play *Twice a Slave* from his friend and fellow historian Dr. Sue Eakin. She
contacted him after reading an article that mentioned he had obtained
the Spring Hill Baptist Church minutes. The minutes had much information on two of its founders: Joseph Willis and William Prince Ford.

Ford had bought the slave Solomon Northup on June 23, 1841, in
New Orleans. He immediately brought him to his Wallfield Plantation.
Just forty-six days later, Joseph Willis and William Prince Ford founded

Spring Hill Baptist Church, on August 8, 1841. Ford's slaves attended the church too, which was the custom in pre-Civil War Louisiana.

The plantation was located on Hurricane Creek, a 1/4 mile east of present-day Forest Hill, Louisiana. It was located on the crest of a hill, on the Texas Road that ran along side a ridge. Northup called this area, in his book *Twelve Years a Slave*, "The Great Piney Woods." Ford was also the headmaster of Spring Creek Academy located near his plantation and Spring Hill Baptist Church. It was there, in 1841, that Joseph Willis would live and entrust his diary to his protégé William Prince Ford, according to historian W.E. Paxton.

✣   ✣   ✣

Ford was not a Baptist preacher when he purchased Solomon Northup and the slave Eliza, a.k.a. Dradey, in 1841, as many books, articles, blogs, and the movie *12 Years a Slave* have portrayed.

The first part of the Spring Hill Baptist Church minutes are written in Ford's own handwriting since he was the first church secretary and also the first church clerk. The minutes reveal that on July 7, 1842, Ford was elected deacon. On December 11, 1842, Ford became the church treasurer, too. It was during the winter of 1842 that Ford sold a 60% share of Northup to John M. Tibeats. Ford's remaining 40% was later conveyed to Edwin Epps, on April 9, 1843.

It was not until February 10, 1844, that Ford was ordained as a Baptist preacher. A year later, on April 12, 1845, Ford was excommunicated for "communing with the Campbellite Church at Cheneyville." But, Ford's later writings reveal that he remained close friends with his neighbor and mentor Joseph Willis.

Dr. Eakin asked Randy if he would help her with her research on William Prince Ford. He also lectured in her history classes, at Louisiana State University at Alexandria, on the subject.

Dr. Eakin wrote Randy Willis on March 7, 1984, "We had a wonderful experience dramatizing Northup and I think there could be a musical play on Joseph Willis. It seems to me it gets the message across far more quickly than routine written material." She added, "a fictional novel based upon Joseph Willis' life would be more interesting to the general public than a biography and would reach a greater audience."

Dr. Eakin is best known for documenting, annotating, and reviving interest in Solomon Northup's 1853 book *Twelve Years a Slave*. She, at the age of eighteen, rediscovered a long-forgotten copy of Solomon Northup's book, on the shelves of a bookstore, near the LSU campus, in Baton Rouge. The bookstore owner sold it to her for only 25 cents. In 2013, *12 Years a Slave* won the Academy Award for Best Picture. In his acceptance speech for the honor, director Steve McQueen thanked Dr. Eakin: "I'd like to thank this amazing historian, Sue Eakin, whose life, she gave her life's work to preserving Solomon's book."

Jim Bowie was a neighbor of Joseph Willis when they both lived near Bayou Chicot. Jim's brother, Rezin Bowie, was a neighbor to Joseph's eldest son Agerton Willis and eldest grandson, Daniel Hubbard Willis Sr., for four years (1824-1827) in the village of Bayou Boeuf. The name changed to Holmesville in 1834, and is located near present-day Eola. It was at Holmesville, on Bayou Boeuf, that Edwin Epps enslaved (1845-1853) Solomon Northup for the last eight years of his twelve year indenture. It was here that Joseph's eldest son and Randy Willis's 3rd great-grandfather Agerton Willis met and married Sophie Story.

In Appreciation

I'm thankful to the many people from the past that have encouraged me to write this story, beginning with my first-cousin Donnie Willis. He planted the first seed in my mind to write about our fourth great-grandfather Joseph Willis. Our sainted grandmother, Lillie Hanks Willis, had a treasure chest of stories about Joseph, and insisted I write them down.

Our Willis family has been blessed with storytellers. My cousin Kimberly Willis Holt is an example of that. Her books have inspired me. I have used her grandfather and my Uncle Howard Willis's arsenal of stories all my life, including in this book.

My cousin, and maternal great-grandson of Joseph, Dr. Greene Wallace Strother gave me all of his vast research. His uncle, Polk Willis, tended to Joseph in his final years, and shared all that he said to Dr. Strother.

My fellow historian and friend, Dr. Sue Eakin asks me to help her with her research on William Prince Ford. I learned much about William Prince Ford and Solomon Northup from her. All of them, except Donnie and Kimberly, are in Heaven now.

Karon McCartney, Archivist at the Louisiana Baptist Convention, has provided much help in organizing, cataloging, and protecting my research for decades, at the Louisiana Baptist Building in Alexandria.

Dr. D. "Pete" Royer Richardson (Associate Professor of Theater with Louisiana College), provided invaluable help with the Cajun French recipes in the novel. She also helped with the costumes used in the photographs for the novel. Jeff Young (Assistant Professor of Media Production with Louisiana College), coordinated the Louisiana College students that were photographed at Melrose Plantation. Jeff and the students trekked to Melrose Plantation, in costume, to participate in the photo shoot. The students were: Grace Carson, Connor Chaffin, Jesse Gallegos, Alex Newell, Rose Smoak, and Brandon Watkins. The cover for the novel was created by Jacob Jolibois. He is a photographer, designer, and writer based out of Baton Rouge.

The photographs may be seen at WWW.THREEWINDSBLOWING.COM

I would like to thank Melrose Plantation, and the Association for the Preservation of Historic Natchitoches' Board of Directors for their hospitality and allowing the use of the image of their beautiful house museum for this novel. Scenes on the cover and website were photographed at Melrose Plantation. It is an Antebellum historic house, museum, and complex of nine buildings located in Natchitoches Parish, Louisiana. It is a National Historic Landmark, owned and operated by the Association for the Preservation of Historic Natchitoches, a non-profit organization. In visiting Melrose, you will discover the rich two-hundred year history of the Plantation. You will learn how the family of a former slave became the legacy of the Cane River Creole community that is still vibrant today. You will also see the impact of the American Civil War on it. You can explore the wonders of the early 20th Century Melrose Artists' Retreat founded by Carmelite "Cammie" Garrett Henry and follow the discovery of Clementine Hunter, one-time Melrose cook, as she emerged to become Louisiana's most celebrated folk artist. To learn more or plan your visit please visit melroseplantation.org or call 318-379-0055.

About the Author

Randy Willis is the author of *Three Winds Blowing, The Apostle to the Opelousas, The Story of Joseph Willis*, and is co-author of *Twice a Slave*. *Twice a Slave* has been chosen as a part of the Jerry B. Jenkins Select Line, along with four bestselling authors. Jerry Jenkins is author of more than 180 books with sales of more than 70 million copies, including the best-selling *Left Behind* series. *Twice a Slave* has been adapted into a dramatic play at Louisiana College, by Dr. D. "Pete" Richardson (Associate Professor of Theater with Louisiana College).

He owns Randy Willis Music Publishing (an ASCAP-affiliated music publishing company), and Town Lake Music Publishing, LLC (a BMI-affiliated music publishing company). He is an ASCAP-affiliated songwriter, and is President of Quadra Record Company.

He is the founder of Operation Warm Heart which feeds and clothes the homeless, and is a member of the Board of Directors of Our Mission Possible (empowering at-risk teens to discover their greatness) in Austin, Texas. He is a member of the Board of Trustees of the Joseph Willis Institute at Louisiana College.

Randy was born in Oakdale, Louisiana, and lived near Forest Hill and Longleaf, Louisiana, as a boy. He currently resides in the Texas Hill Country. He graduated from Angleton High School in Angleton, Texas, and Texas State University in San Marcos, Texas, with a BBA. He was a graduate student at Texas State University. He is single and the father of three sons and has four grandchildren.

He is a fourth great-grandson of Joseph Willis, and his foremost historian.

To learn more about the author, characters and animals in this book visit:

WWW.THREEWINDSBLOWING.COM